DESIRES UNLEASHED

What Reviewers Say About
Renee Roman's Work

Where the Lies Hide

"I like the concept of the novel. The story idea is well thought out and well researched. I really connected with Cam's character…"—*Rainbow Reflections*

"[T]his book is just what I needed. There's plenty of romantic tension, intrigue, and mystery. I wanted Sarah to find her brother as much as she did, and I struggled right alongside Cam in her discoveries."—*Kissing Backwards*

"Overall, a really great novel. Well written incredible characters, an interesting investigation storyline and the perfect amount of sexy times."—*Books, Life and Everything Nice*

"This is a fire and ice romance wrapped up in an engaging crime plot that will keep you hooked."—*Istoria Lit*

Epicurean Delights

"[*Epicurean Delights*] is captivating, with delightful humor and well-placed banter taking place between the two characters. …[T]he main characters are lovable and easily become friends we'd like to see succeed in life and in love."—*Lambda Literary Review*

By the Author

Epicurean Delights

Stroke of Fate

Hard Body

Where the Lies Hide

Bonded Love

Body Language

Hot Days, Heated Nights

Escorted

Glass and Stone

Desires Unleashed

DESIRES UNLEASHED

by
Renee Roman

2023

DESIRES UNLEASHED
© 2023 By Renee Roman. All Rights Reserved.

ISBN 13: 978-1-63679-327-6

This Trade Paperback Original Is Published By
Bold Strokes Books, Inc.
P.O. Box 249
Valley Falls, NY 12185

First Edition: February 2023

Credits
Editor: Cindy Cresap
Production Design: Susan Ramundo
Cover Design By Tammy Seidick

Acknowledgments

This book started as a way to encourage exploration of finding one's authentic self and the many desires we keep hidden away for fear of ridicule and societal preconceptions of what our lives should look like.

It's not an easy task to thank those who have helped me up when I've stumbled or given words of encouragement or shared a smile or kind word when I've needed it most, but I'm going to try.

To JW…for your patience and guidance in showing me the world of BDSM and its tenets which are vital to this story. My questions were many and my gratitude is vast. I hope I've made you proud.

My beta reader, Tony. Decades of knowledge were shared, comparing old school ways and making room for the new. Thank you for your feedback.

Cindy Cresap, editor extraordinaire. I've had the privilege of your immense editing and writing knowledge from the start, and I'm so happy we can continue the journey together. Thanks for your praise, encouragement, and the comments that make me smile. They mean the world to me.

Sandy Lowe, the go-to person in all things that books are made of. Thank you for help with the blurbs I despise writing, and the great ideas of how to make my stories better.

Radclyffe, the heart of Bold Strokes Books. Thank you for having a dream and for sharing it with the world. I'm forever grateful for your vision, insight, and the courage to go after what you wanted. You've encouraged me, and authors (and future authors) to do the same.

To readers who have stuck by me through the early bumps as I maneuvered the road to learning this craft we call writing, "Thank you" can't truly express how much I appreciate your support. Being an author can be a lonely existence. Knowing you are waiting for more helps the process feel less so.

Dedication

For the BDSM community and the Kinksters of the world.
Safe, sane, consensual are the tenets by which you live.
I honor and respect the open communication
and the code of honor by which you live.

Choose to live your life to the fullest.
Always.

CHAPTER ONE

I stared at the nameplate facing me. *Kell Murphy, Operations Manager.* My name was used so many times through the course of a day I'd seriously considered changing it, more than once. I pulled my day planner closer and scanned the page of neatly scripted entries, though it wasn't necessary. I knew each item that needed to be addressed before the end of each workday, whenever that happened to be. It would be at least several hours before I finished, and my energy level was already lagging. A double shot of espresso in my favorite latte might provide the jolt I needed. Just as I stood, the phone rang and I rolled my eyes. Wasn't that always the way?

"Murphy."

"Johnson here. I just got off the phone with an irate guest who swore the front desk clerks were, and I quote, 'A bunch of befuddled baboons who would be more entertaining at the zoo,' end quote."

Pinching the bridge of my nose didn't help, but it did stop me from leading in with a string of oaths. The regional manager of Oasis Hotels wouldn't be on the phone if the situation didn't warrant an intervention. There'd be no trip to Starbucks in my immediate future, especially if I didn't take care of the issue I was sure to hear about. "Did they say who the most offensive baboon was?"

"Funny. Let me see," Johnson said before the sound of rustling papers filled the silence. "The cheeky redhead with the too bright smile. I wrote it down to make sure I had it right."

Great. Samantha was in for a little one-on-one time in my office. I made a point of getting to the bottom of any complaint as soon as possible before memories blurred and denials could be formulated. "Send me the folio of the guest and I'll take care of it on my end."

"I know you will, Kell. That's why I hired you. Let me know how it goes."

"Will do." Not being the HR person for the corporation left me a little wiggle room. Not enough to have a complaint lodged, but definitely enough to get my point across in no uncertain terms. The clock taunted me. Without questioning the wisdom of my actions, I grabbed my phone and took off, my box-heeled shoes making distinct clicks as I hustled down the less affluent and slightly creepy stairwell. My destination was only a block away. If I was going to put on my no-nonsense persona, caffeine was not only desired, but necessary. Some days I hated my job, but not today. Today I was going to right a wrong perception of what qualified as a good employee. Staff were being paid to treat *all* customers, in no uncertain terms, as valued guests. I was happy I didn't have to deal with the same issues when I bartended. The only annoyance there was the occasional inebriated patron, and so far I'd found them to be comical rather than a pain in the ass.

When I banged open the door to the street, my eyes watered from the abundant sunshine that greeted me. I took a breath while my eyes adjusted, then smiled. The opportunity to escape the gorgeous resort didn't happen often, but I'd learned to appreciate those rare moments when I could. The expansive grounds were a self-contained oasis in the middle of an over-developed downtown area, a hidden gem amongst the concrete towers and street level shops. It was the best—and the worst—of both worlds.

As I reached the main thoroughfare, four lanes of traffic buzzed by, and pedestrians meandered in both directions, unaware of the tense conversation I'd been submerged in a few short minutes ago. I strode inside the café of my guilty indulgence, ordered a dirty chai latte, and added a generous tip because I knew the barista had to put up with a lot of shit throughout the day, sometimes more than I did. It was all I could do to wait until I got outside to take that first glorious sip in mental preparation for the face-off that would happen once Samantha was seated in front of me.

❖

"Taylor Simpson."

"Ms. Simpson, this is Mrs. Abernathy's chauffer, Jackson. Are your appointments running on time?"

The hair at the back of my neck bristled. "Of course."

"Excellent. We'll be there in five minutes."

I swore under my breath for the umpteenth time in the last six hours. As the events coordinator and part owner of the business, I took on a lion's share of the hard-to-pull-off affairs. That usually meant weddings and family reunions because they were often wrought with last-minute changes, hysterical clients, and a shit storm of coordinating the many and varied vendors, all of which I somehow managed to blend into a seemingly well-choreographed display of outrageously overpriced services, mine not excluded. Today though, was fated to try my usual well-groomed patience. Thanks to the universe, I had a way to destress later, otherwise my staff and everyone else around me would feel the wrath of a boss on the warpath.

In my en suite bathroom, I took advantage of the luxury of having something meant for me alone and gave my attire the once-over. My suit was a classic cut from the finest silk available and the price tag proved it. Not one to normally quibble over such necessities, even I had balked at the outrageous cost. Lucky for me, I got to write off a percentage on my taxes, otherwise it might be off the rack for me, and that would never do if I wanted well-off clients to continue to demand our services. A put-together individual spoke of confidence and an awareness for details, two things that were a must in the business. I gave a nod to the mirror, picked up the binder labeled "Abernathy" off the corner of my desk, and strode with purpose to planning room two. Such was my fate.

"Welcome to At Your Service. I'm Taylor Simpson, your event coordinator," I said as a way of introduction to the two women seated at the round table where a tray of refreshments took up the center. "It's a pleasure to meet you, Ms. Abernathy." I extended my hand to the young woman who appeared more than a little nervous. We'd spoken on the phone several times in the last month. In those instances, she sounded confident in regard to what she wanted, but I suppose sounding and looking could be two very different things.

"Likewise, Ms. Simpson. I'd like to introduce my mother, Victoria Abernathy."

I nodded and smiled, a requisite rather than a sentiment as the mother of the bride gave me the once-over, including a raised brow that might or might not bode well for setting the tone. If she thought I could be intimidated she was sadly mistaken. I shook her hand, and the idea that she might be confused by the blue polish on my short but well-manicured nails almost made me laugh out loud.

My true nature was to take control and lead in no uncertain terms, and she'd find out soon enough that she'd hired not only the best for her daughter's wedding, but someone who wouldn't put up with haughty behavior. I settled in my seat, uncapped my pen, and opened the binder. "Shall we begin?"

Two hours and the start of a migraine later, I walked the Abernathys to the elevator, assuring them everything would go according to plan. The daughter would be easy enough to work with. I handled obedient women in most settings, and she'd been raised with an obvious iron hand. Not the method I used, but effective enough if desired. The mother was another story. Let's just say she was not only cut from a different fabric, but she was also the whole bolt and used to getting her way. So was I. A war of wills had ensued from the beginning, and I'd had all I could do to not let my sometimes-volatile temper win out. This was not the place to display my Dominant side, and I congratulated myself for having the wherewithal to maintain my composure.

I'd have an opportunity to shine through later and instead focused my attention on the details I'd recorded in the binder. Computers were fine for some tasks, but for the constant updates, changes, and notes that would be added regarding each vendor, the event timeline, and other crucial tasks, I still found pen to paper, with the addition of a pack of sticky notes, my go-to. Call me old-fashioned, but I liked applying my hand to the visible record.

Like my handprint on a presented ass, leaving my mark gave me more pleasure than some of the more obvious ones the vanilla world was so fond of pursuing. The accompanying moan was not to be overlooked either. The business was my daytime setting where I earned my bread and butter, though I couldn't control a lot of what happened, and instead bowed to the whims of my clientele. Not a position I liked at all. When I attended kink events where I wasn't held back by the social restraints of decorum and was free to let my metaphorical hair down, there were no restrains or resistance to what I wanted. If it were up to me, I'd live the lifestyle twenty-four/seven. Unfortunately, that wasn't my current situation, but someday it would be if the right partner ever came along.

Chapter Two

You wanted to see me, Ms. Murphy?"
Samantha stood in front of my desk looking for all the world like the epitome of an exemplary employee—hands clasped in front of her, making steady eye contact, and her uniform jacket neatly pressed. She'd been at the resort for less than six months and during that she'd settled in to her front desk position with enthusiasm. Samantha was vivacious in a way that many would find annoying, but that's not how I saw it at all. In today's work force, finding an enthusiastic employee was rare, and I liked that she understood she'd have to work her way up the food chain through dedication and hard work. The incident they were about to discuss seemed out of character, and I wanted to know why. Most of the time, she lived up to her reputation, but every once in a while her bratty nature showed through, and those were the times I did the job I was expected to do. A controlled, stress-filled, albeit, well-paid one. It included running the resort with the utmost attention to detail and getting the very best out of each employee.

Samantha would need to remember I was there to make less work for her. And while I didn't have time to hand hold, I hoped I could handle these type situations with patience. The same rule applied to those moments when my sexual partners, infrequent as they were, needed reassurance and encouragement to take the lead. Maybe I needed to reimagine the kind of woman I sought to share my bed with.

"Hi, Samantha. Have a seat." I indicated one of the medium comfort chairs facing me. The kind that was comfortable enough for guests and employees alike though I hoped not so comfortable that they'd make a habit of sitting here. I took off my glasses and swung the monitor out of my way so I wouldn't be distracted by incoming emails. "I received a call this morning from upstairs." Everyone knew the term meant it was from someone higher than me, and that was rarely a good thing.

"Oh." Samantha's face fell. "I assume that means it had something to do with me?"

At least she had the gumption to ask. It was one of the things I liked about her. She might be young and somewhat inexperienced, but she was also upfront and didn't make excuses.

I nodded. I needed to choose my words carefully. Every business was scrambling to fill vacancies, and I didn't want to have one more on my hands. Who knew. Maybe someday Samantha would be sitting where I am now. To get there she'd have to learn how to cultivate employees to get the most from them, and I believed the best way to teach someone was to set an example. "Do you remember having a recent discussion with a guest that might have been interpreted as unprofessional?" Her lips pursed, revealing I didn't need to use a name to jog her memory.

"If you're talking about Ms. Mahoney, then yes. She requested a full refund because the bed, to use her paraphrase, 'Was so worn and uncomfortable I hardly slept at all. My back will never be the same.'"

"I see." Bratty attitude or not, Samantha wasn't one to easily become riled and I wanted all the facts. "What was your response?" From where I sat, it was clear she was going over the conversation in her head.

"I told her I was sorry she'd not gotten rest and that she should have called to have her room, or the mattress, changed. She huffed at the suggestion." Samantha tipped her head as though retrieving more bits of information from her memory bank. "I checked her file. She'd made five other complaints during her three-night stay. She was bucking for a free vacation and her complaints didn't warrant it."

The documentation I had access to included the lifetime dossier of Janet Mahoney, along with a detailed string of demands during each stay. The woman was rich *and* conniving, and likely believed if she barked loud enough, she'd get her way. In light of the facts, Samantha's response was reasonable, but that didn't serve as an excuse for not bringing the matter to my attention immediately.

"As in a previous incident earlier this year, I wish you would have contacted me while our guest was present. There are concessions I may or may not make depending on the specific circumstances, but it's my job to handle those type of complaints. If I had been made aware then, it would have never gotten as far as it did, and you wouldn't be sitting here now."

"Yes, Ms. Murphy." Samantha looked chagrined; her cheeks shaded pink.

"You're a valuable employee, Samantha, and I know you put up with complaints on a daily basis. You have to trust that I'll do my job when a guest becomes escalated. In turn I'll make sure you have the opportunity to do yours." I watched as Samantha's lower lip trembled and a part of me regretted making her feel bad. I softened my gaze. "I'll take care of Ms. Mahoney. You didn't do anything wrong, but you also shouldn't have to deal with people bent on making your job more difficult than it already is." I needed to make sure she knew I was on her side. "I'm here to help make each day as pleasant as it can be. I can't do that if I don't know there's a problem." I stood and held out my hand. There was no purpose to browbeating her. Ms. Mahoney was a PIA any way you looked at the situation.

Samantha rose, a tentative smile on her face. "Yes, ma'am. I'll remember."

I extended my hand and when Samantha took it, I covered hers in one of mine. "I'm sorry I had to call you into my office, but I'm glad I know what happened. Please don't hesitate to trust I'm here to help you, Samantha." I smiled warmly as I remembered my early days at the resort. The person who I replaced had little in the way of people skills and if it hadn't been for Johnson being on site for a management conference I doubt I would have been considered for the promotion. That sequence of events led me to be the kind of supervisor I was today. I cared about my employees and wanted to be sure they knew it.

Samantha quietly closed the door behind her, and I was confident she wouldn't hesitate to let me step in on her behalf the next time a guest was unreasonable. If not, our next meeting might not be as pleasant and that was something I hoped wouldn't happen.

I shook my mouse and woke up the screen, then dialed the number listed. It was time to make nice with Ms. Mahoney, even if it was the last thing she deserved.

❖

"You sure do serve up a mean Manhattan, Kell."

I smiled at the now-familiar patron midway down the bar. "Thanks, Jack. Glad you approve." His eyes were kind, full of understanding from having witnessed too many things. Joy, sorrow, and pain to name just a few. The crow's-feet at the corners of his eyes spoke of hours of smiling, but I wondered if much made him smile anymore. He was melancholy more than jovial, though he always had a wink and a nod for me.

I emptied dregs from beer bottles and dropped them in the nearly filled case. The glasses stacked on the lower counter were next. A sink of hot soapy water with a stiff brush shaped like a U that would clean both the inside and outer edge of the glass was sticking partway out of the water. The rapid up and down movement removed any residual lipstick, prints, or whatever else might linger, followed by a couple of quick dips in equally hot water to rinse the suds away. I flipped each one onto the rubber drying mat.

"What's new in your world?" I asked then looked up because Jack seemed like he wanted someone to talk to.

"You mean aside from a job I can't stand and a wife I can't keep happy?" Jack winked in my direction. "Not a damn thing."

I paused long enough to share an empathetic smile before getting back to the continuous to-do list. I didn't mind being busy at all. The purpose for taking this job wasn't hard to understand. Each shift allowed me the undeniable pleasure of not having to think, just do. The methodical tasks were a nice break from the constant demands of controlling what the staff was doing, or not doing, which created the kind of stress and anxiety I longed to escape. I was more than happy to relinquish control outside my day job, in fact, it was what had driven me in such a divergent direction in the first place.

I needed a break from autonomy. For someone else to be in charge and drive things, handle situations that arose. Somewhere I could step away and not worry about repercussions. I wanted the freedom to not be the "go-to" except for something as simple as providing the service of making a decent drink, sharing bad jokes, and listening to how much life sucked for the person on the other side of the bar. It was like watching a live soap opera play out in real time and I often grinned. It came naturally because most of the stuff I heard was funny. As in "you can't make this shit up" funny. The telltale squeak of the front door made me look up. A woman confidently strode in and sat in the same place she'd sat in for the past several weeks, whenever she came in.

"Good evening. What can I get you?" The woman hadn't shared her name and she hadn't ordered the same thing to drink or eat since I had seen her the first time.

"A dry martini, two olives, shaken not stirred, and an order of bruschetta." The woman's smile was warm even if her words were bland and without inflection. Tonight, she wore a black, form-fitting oxford shirt that hinted at small, high breasts.

"You got it." For all the elements of an old, neighborhood bar that remained, the Water Hole had a modern ordering system, an updated satellite network, and a sparkling kitchen. They were all part of the reason I'd chosen this place over the dozens of others spread throughout the downtown area. I typed in the food order and began making the drink. I set it on the requisite cocktail napkin without spilling a drop. It had taken me a bit to master that particular skill.

The woman took a sip, held it a minute, then swallowed. "Excellent," she said before making eye contact. "Thank you, Kell."

My surprise was likely displayed on my face. "You're welcome. You seem to have the advantage of knowing my name though I don't know yours."

"Does that mean you won't be serving me perfect drinks anymore if you don't find out?" She flashed another friendly smile.

"I'll still serve you," I said, enjoying the light banter between us. I wasn't in any hurry for it to end. "But it might not be as good." It was all I could do to keep from grinning and in the effort, my mouth twitched.

"I see." The woman's face remained impassive and for a brief time I wondered if I'd overplayed my hand, but then she stood, and her blue eyes held mine with such surety I couldn't help moving toward her.

"Taylor," she said as she extended her hand, the dark blue nail polish, a counterpoint to her presentation, emphasized the color of her eyes and reflected the overhead lights. "I prefer the pronouns of she/they/them."

Without any hesitation I reached out, and she firmly grasped my hand. Like everything else about Taylor, the strength of her grip was certain and with enough pressure to relay she was in control of the greeting. "Nice to meet you, Taylor." She held on for a few ticks past a friendly handshake before letting go.

Taylor resumed her seat. "Are you new to the area?"

The line was rather cliché, though I didn't get the feeling that's how it was meant. "I've lived here about six years." I wiped the bar even though it didn't need it. It gave me time to consider how much I wanted to share.

"Do you like what you do?"

I glanced up to see Taylor sipping her cocktail as she studied me as though I were a mystery she wanted to unravel. It both excited and unnerved me. "You mean bartending?"

"Yes."

The kitchen bell rang, and I was grateful to move away from the intensity of her gaze. I set the plate down along with utensils in a linen napkin, hoping she'd let the question hang.

"Do you?" Taylor unwrapped her silverware, her focus on me never wavering.

I pulled a bottle of water from the cooler, anything to keep my hands busy, unsure why she had such a rattling effect on me. "It's a nice change from my day job." After cracking the seal, I took a long drink and hoped the ice-cold liquid would cool the simmer of attraction inside.

"What else do you do?" Taylor cut a slice of bruschetta in half before taking a bite. Somehow she managed it without the toppings tumbling off, a skill I hadn't mastered no matter how many times I tried.

The conversation wasn't going as I'd hoped when I started the innocent flirting, and now I had to decide whether to continue or abandon it altogether. Neither felt viable, so I went with the truth. "I'm not sure I want to tell you more since we've only just met."

"Do you think I'll stalk you?"

Her assessment about my reluctance, though somewhat accurate, rubbed me the wrong way. "I don't know you well enough to answer yes or no."

Taylor zeroed in on my eyes. "No, you don't, but if you want to I'll need to know about you, too."

The frank response took me aback. I wanted to tell her to stick her analytical bullshit where the sun doesn't shine, but her honesty was refreshing, and I was further drawn in. I wasn't about to give her the satisfaction of hearing me admit it though. "Perhaps, but that's not going to happen tonight."

Taylor went back to her food. "May I have a bottle of water?"

The change of subject was disappointing, but I hid it behind a facade of indifference and placed the bottle in front of her as she ate the last of the bruschetta and finished it off with what remained of her cocktail. I updated her bill and slid it into the tumbler at the edge of the bar, removed the dishes, and brought them to the kitchen where Maggie asked if the customer liked the food. My face heated. I hadn't even bothered to ask. "It's gone, isn't it?" I laughed and so did Maggie. When I returned to the bar, Taylor was gone. Money, including a generous tip, sat in the glass. I snatched the bills and the tab, then noticed writing on the back.

If you ever want to learn about trust, you have to be willing to share.

I glanced up in time to see Taylor standing outside of the plate glass window. Her mouth moved into a sensual, knowing smile. My heart beat faster in response, and suddenly I wanted to know everything about her and wondered how much of herself she'd actually be willing to share.

CHAPTER THREE

The narrow staircase lit by flickering electric torches closed around me like a comforting cocoon. This was so much like home, I often wondered if I should build a house of my own designed with all the pertinent elements that were contained in one of my favorite places to fully be me.

"Dark Heat, welcome."

"Thank you," I said, briefly considering changing my BDSM handle. I flashed my driver's license with my legal name. Taylor Simpson didn't exist here, even if she was a necessary part of my daytime persona.

The guard at the door exchanged the ten-dollar entrance fee for a drink ticket. The minimal cost to participate went for equipment purchases and maintenance, along with the supplies for keeping everything sanitary and safe to use. I gripped my implement bag and moved down the hall before stepping into the well-lit, cavernous space. The Play Palace was my favorite members-only dungeon, and I was more than ready to play. Kell's innocent curiosity had been tempered by an appreciative amount of caution, and the combination had not only made her all the more interesting but had primed me for an intense scene. Now all I had to do was find a willing play partner.

After tucking the ticket in my back pocket, I grabbed a bottle of water from the plastic tubs strategically placed among equipment, leather couches, and other play areas. Wednesday nights weren't as popular as the weekend, which suited me. I preferred to not be jammed up against bodies I didn't know, and it was difficult to adhere to the no touching rule when there was scant room to move. My gaze traveled over several familiar faces, none of whom I wanted to engage with. Perhaps I wouldn't get to play after all.

"Dark Heat." The voice behind me was both familiar and arousing.

I turned to find a play partner I hadn't seen in a while. She didn't cruise the familiar online social networks and we'd never exchanged personal information, but I knew her, nonetheless. I attributed her absence to one of a million reasons and left it at that. The nice thing about the lifestyle was there were always people to play with if they suited what I wanted, and stalking was frowned upon.

"SoftandEasy, it's been a while."

She nodded before sipping from the bottle of water she held, her name written in bold letters on a white label. "Yeah, well, you know how it goes."

Then I remembered the reason for her absence. A while back, she'd gotten caught up in a bad scene. It didn't happen often, but when it did sometimes it took a while to come back from it. "You doing all right?"

She ran a hand through her long, straight blond strands. "It's my first time here since…" She didn't need to finish. I'd witnessed the beating and had been one of the first to step in with a dozen more kinksters beside me. It was a prime example of a scene gone wrong. The altercation became scary for everyone.

I'm sure she had carried the visible scars for a while and the mental ones likely still lingered, but I was glad to see her.

"Can I hug you?"

Soft blew out a harsh breath. "I wish you would." She stepped into my arms, sighed, and instantly relaxed. I was glad to provide a place she could feel safe in. As a Dominant, I took the responsibility seriously, and even though we hadn't played in a long time I cared about Soft, like I cared about all of my play partners. Those feelings were not on the same level as a dynamic, but I couldn't—wouldn't—engage with a play partner without at least liking them while sharing some of the same morals and philosophies I held to.

"Thank you," Soft whispered in my ear before she stepped back, her eyes glassy. "Do you have a scene tonight?" She motioned to the bartender and tossed her ticket and a five-dollar bill on the bar. Her signature tequila sunrise appeared a few minutes later.

"Not yet." I tempered my smile, unsure if she was offering. "But I'm hopeful."

Her cheeks darkened and her eyes darted away. When she glanced up she looked sad. "I can't…"

"Hey," I said, covering her fisted hand with mine. "Don't apologize. It's good to see you. The rest…" I shrugged. "Is an extension of our friendship."

She nodded at the sentiment. "Thanks."

I meant it. SoftandEasy had a beautiful soul whose only desire had ever been one of service to the Dominant she was with. Knowing someone had put out that flame had pissed me off. Still did. We stood in relative silence and watched a few play partners engaged in various acts. Their obvious joy only ramped up my need, and my clit grew exponentially.

She finished her drink, then shoved a hand in her tight black jeans. "I'm going to call it a night. At least I can walk in here without wanting to vomit." She laughed, though I could tell it was bittersweet.

I pulled her in for another hug, holding her close with my palm on the nape of her neck. It was an intimate move that I used with submissives whom I was tightly bound with, and while we'd never been in a long-lasting dynamic, we'd played enough times that I felt a kindred spirit with Soft, and she needed the tender gesture. Needed to know I cared.

She stepped out of my embrace and her smile appeared genuine this time. "Thank you."

"You're welcome." There wasn't much else I could do or say, and elaborating would have only made our interaction feel stilted. Soft deserved respect not patronization.

"See you around." As she walked through the crowd toward the exit she held her head high.

I sent out a silent wish for her well-being, finished the water, and picked up my bag. It was time to satisfy the urge that never really left, only simmered in the background while I was in my vanilla world. It was my constant companion, and the need to dominate was a living, breathing part of who I was, and it was hungry. The open lounge area served as hunting ground, filled with like-minded Dominants and submissives ready to serve. All were there for the taking or giving, depending on their role. I knew mine, and I needed to find someone who knew theirs. I wouldn't settle for less.

A vision came in mid-stride, and I stopped abruptly. Kell's flushed cheeks and demure glance flashed in my mind. Would she be interested in knowing me if my true nature was revealed? Would she be willing to submit? Did she even know how that would feel?

I shook my head. The uncharacteristic wondering would have to wait. Kell wasn't here and maybe she never would be, but I knew what I wanted and how I wanted it as the weight of my duffel pulled me farther into the space. For tonight I'd concentrate on who *was* available, and in that moment, no one else mattered. No one at all.

❖

In It To Win was a Switch I'd watched a few times. They were confident in both roles, and I'd never seen them slide from one persona to another in a scene. At the moment, they had their plump lips wrapped around the head of my cock. It wasn't my biggest by far, but it was the one I chose for tonight. "Be a good girl," I said as I began slowly pushing deeper in short thrusts. I backed out until only my head was hidden in their mouth and their eyes flicked up at me in challenge or want. I grabbed their hair and held their head as I pushed my cock all the way in. Its gaze never wavered as the gag reflex won out, then they appeared to relax into the cock shoved in their throat. I'm sure they would have smiled if they didn't have a mouthful. My clit pounded behind the base of my cock. This was what I wanted, needed. Receiving total submission was my power. When I looked down, Kell's face was there. She smiled at me. I wasn't ready for the force of her blatant desire that reached so deep I stepped back to the wall before ripping off the harness that suddenly felt too tight, too restrictive. In It moved forward on their knees before hesitating, still holding the pose I'd moved them into when we started.

"Master?"

I rarely needed physical release when I played with a submissive. "Head." I wanted them to give me head, needed to feel their lips around my hard clit. They stopped inches from my thighs. Suddenly the only thing that mattered was getting off. After I widened my stance, In It came closer and buried their face in my crotch, lips wrapped around my throbbing center. This time when I face fucked them, I closed my eyes and let another's fill my vision. My hips thrust harder, my breathing harsh before I exploded in a groan, covering their chin and chest with my cum. Shock could have ruined the moment because it was rare I came so hard I squirted, but the absence of being surprised only served to fuel a greater need. One that *did* surprise me, and I had no way of ever knowing if I'd have it satisfied, but a plan formulated around how I'd find out.

CHAPTER FOUR

I sipped my martini between bites of the flatbread pizza with arugula, mozzarella, and blistered tomatoes. The sweet potato fries were my guilty indulgence and I tried to limit those to one order per week. Of course, alcohol didn't count.

"How's the bartending going, Kell?" Dee, a friend who I'd met at the resort a half-dozen years ago, asked as she crunched calamari.

"It's great, and a nice change from the resort."

Dee nodded knowingly. We talked once a week and she'd become one of my closest friends. I'd told her about doing something on the side. Not for the money, but for the change in scenery and responsibilities. I didn't hate my job, but there were times when I questioned how long I could continue in the hospitality industry when there were days I didn't feel hospitable at all. She said I had the personality for bartending. I'd laughed at first, but when I heard a local bar was looking for someone to fill in, I talked to the owner and he offered me the job with the stipulation that I attend a bartending class that ran Monday, Wednesday, Friday for four weeks. I'd never had so much fun in any class until then.

"Would it be okay if I stopped in to see you some night? I've always wanted to go to the Water Hole, but…" She shrugged.

The bar was a far cry from the upscale places the group frequented, including tonight's choice. The fancy chandeliers hanging from the vaulted ceiling sparkled and spoke of the high prices they charged. I preferred the simple warmth of the Hole. "Of course you can. I'd love to mix you up one of my specialties."

Dee nodded. "Great. You work Wednesdays?"

"Until next week," I said. "One of the full-time bartenders put in his notice and the night shift folks are picking up the vacancies for the foreseeable future. That means I'll be there Fridays and Sundays too for a while." Dee was about to comment, but Karen's strident voice cut her off.

"So, I said to Larry, 'If you're gonna gag every time your son fills a diaper you better be first in line for toilet training.'" Laughter traveled around the table following the quip, and a few shared similar comments and sentiments ensued.

I smiled, not knowing what it must be like to be a parent, though I could commiserate about being in a one-sided relationship. "I don't know how you do it." Groans and headshakes came from all the married women. I meant it. My life was already complicated with some days not having any free time at all. A long day at the resort followed by bartending, soon to be three times a week for a while, gave me a reason to be grateful the procreation urges never chased me.

"Honestly, Kell, you're so organized, I think you should give parenthood a try."

"Don't even suggest that!" Children were meant to be adored from afar, or promptly returned to their parents following a limited-engagement playdate. I didn't have a repulsion for them. I just didn't see myself as the parent type. This wasn't the first time my hetero friends had talked about my producing a screamer, and when I played the gay card, their comeback was, "That's no excuse." True, but it didn't change my mind.

"Suit yourself, but it's not all sleepless nights and poverty you know." Karen, the youngest of the group who had somehow managed to have three children before she was twenty-five, never gave up the "don't knock it till you try it" theme.

I was going to go the "With my job, when would I ever see them" route, but that wasn't the reason at all. As the youngest of four children, I'd had to claw and scrape for my parents' attention and the idea that I might choose to ignore my own child was all the reason I needed. Besides, a child would be one more responsibility I had no interest in bearing, including a lifetime commitment with at least eighteen years of trying to control someone who depended on me to make good decisions for them while they rebelled against each one.

If I didn't love my job as much as anyone could by selling their soul for a paycheck, I'd likely walk away from it. I liked my comfortable existence too much to give it up. I'd never be rich, but I was financially stable enough to be able to take vacations, when I could get the time, and enjoy delicious meals at upscale restaurants. I glanced up to find everyone looking in my direction and I couldn't help thinking this was one more group of people who wanted direction from me that I wasn't willing to give. Finally, Maggie spoke up.

"Coffee?" she asked as the waiter caught her signal to remove our plates and start clearing the table.

In that moment I longed to be somewhere else. In the company of someone who wasn't afraid to take control of a situation. The vision of Taylor's confident smile flashed before me, and the wet heat that followed made me shiver. Taylor acted like a woman who enjoyed taking the reins. What was her story? Why did she come to the bar every Wednesday and where did she go afterward? Did she have a partner? A lover? Questions swirled like a whirlpool churning in on itself and disappearing unanswered. Four more days until my next shift at the bar. Four more days until I saw Taylor again. Four more days to find the courage to ask about the cryptic message she'd left and what it meant.

❖

It was very late, and I was tired. The girls had badgered me into going for a nightcap which turned into two. Apparently, they weren't in any hurry to get home to their precious children and inattentive husbands after all. I had no such aversion to being home, wanting nothing more than a hot shower before crawling into my ridiculously comfortable bed, where I gave in to exhaustion. I enjoyed their company, and it would be months before everyone's schedule would match up for another night out.

The stories they shared, some of which were downright hilarious, got me thinking about how much soap operas were shaped after real life even though they were an exaggerated version of it. The sharing of the antics my friends went through gave me an opportunity to reexamine the intricacies of their relationships and how it intersected and played out in their lives. Sadness enveloped me. Brenda and I had never had that type of a relationship, and why, after all this time thoughts of our failure to find a rhythm still haunted me brought with it an even sadder weight that lay heavy in my heart. Maybe I wasn't relationship material. Too stuck in my ways and in my own head to meet someone halfway had been my "go-to" for as long as I could remember. My siblings had always found the key to manipulating our parents in such a way that they usually gave in to their whims, but I had to fight for every victory, and they weren't always sweet. My parental relationship while growing up had been contentious and a battle of wills. That mindset followed me into adulthood.

Would I ever be able to relinquish the control I'd honed for my personal and professional advancement to another person? Even the idea of letting someone else take the reins sent a not-too-pleasant shiver through me. Whomever she was, she would have to be exceptional. Someone who understood what I needed to survive in my own head while winning my heart. A deep sigh escaped as I fluffed and wriggled to find the perfect spot. The likelihood of meeting a partner was far-fetched. I pounded my pillow into submission out of frustration before finally settling my body, though my thoughts continued to whirl, grasping at imaginary images of a future mate.

The wash of exhaustion, relentless as ocean waves, soon overtook me, and the final picture that floated through my mind was of a woman who already *knew* me, though she hardly knew me at all, nor I them. The last thing I remembered before the darkness of sleep came was how ridiculous it was to be thinking of Taylor.

CHAPTER FIVE

The Abernathy notebook sat open on my desk. Sticky notes stuck out along the edge of pages, ten to be exact. Ten alterations, changes, and tweaks. They weren't unexpected. Almost every wedding I had planned over the past eight years had a few, but it had only been eight days and the changes were mounting, almost guaranteeing to surpass previous weddings by a mile. Of course, most of that had to do with the mother, not my actual client, but since the woman was paying, I had to make sure she was happy, or they'd go elsewhere. Soon it would be too late to make major changes, and I couldn't wait until that time came. I could only imagine what the pages would look like in another week.

A week. That's how long it had been since I'd seen Kell. The same night the scene I'd orchestrated took a turn in a direction I'd been helpless to control and that wasn't what I let happen as a Dom. The only saving grace had been that my play partner hadn't expressed much in the way of boundaries, and it was a good thing too because I'd lost my mind for a few minutes there, demanding to be serviced by oral sex, rather than my silicone phallus. I couldn't remember the last time that had happened, and I didn't want a repeat tonight.

"Derek, can you please bring me the latest numbers for four-tier wedding cakes?"

"Sure, Taylor. It will take me a few minutes though. I'm pulling something together for Les."

I rolled my eyes to the empty office. "First chance you have then." I hung up after Derek promised results. Les, real name Leslie, was my business partner. She was always getting the jump on having the staff do her bidding. Tall and muscular in all the right places, Les turned heads wherever she went. Her jet-black hair and blue eyes, the darkest blue I'd ever seen, got her a lot of things, except for the kind of relationship she never seemed to find. I would have sworn she was part of the kink community, but when I asked if she wanted to join me at the Palace, she'd said it wasn't her thing. Could have fooled me. It wasn't the first time I'd been wrong, but those times were few and far between.

At a temporary standstill for who knew how long, the vision of Kell returned and gave me a reason to consider altering my habit of stopping at the Water Hole before tonight's trip to the Play Palace. I could go somewhere else, but the routine I'd established almost a year ago served as my centering point. A preparatory sequence of events that primed not only my mind but also my body. Now there was a new factor, and Kell wouldn't be as easy to handle as other parts of the usual string of events that served as a warmup for play scenes. I didn't have a date per se, but I never made the trip without finding someone to play with unless I decided that's what *I* wanted.

No matter what happened as far as Kell was concerned, I would be the one to dictate if, or when, or how. There'd never been anyone in my D/s relationships who was capable of getting me to relinquish control. Submissive wasn't who I was, and I was as certain of that as I was Kell had no idea how much she wanted to be mine.

❖

Kell glanced at the door when I entered and her back stiffened. The note I'd left her was meant to stir her curiosity. Whether it had the desired effect or not, I had an inkling tonight I'd find out. After settling onto my usual stool, I made eye contact and waited for Kell's response. She took a breath and approached, her shoulders tense and her smile reserved. Being tentative was a trait of a novice sub and my center stirred.

"Hi. What can I get you?" She wiped the already gleaming bar.

"Arancini and something smokey to drink." I was about to open a proverbial door, but Kell had no way of knowing the implications. "What do you recommend?"

Her eyebrow shot up and a slow smile formed. "I've got just the thing." Kell called the food order in as she pulled bottles from the shelf behind her and filled a shaker with ice. She measured a few liquors, one after the other, into a shot glass but she moved too fast for me to see the labels. Once all the alcohol had been poured, she added a sprinkle of cinnamon, a little agave, and another ingredient I couldn't see from where I sat. She swirled the shaker in a stirring motion, ran a slice of lime around the rim of a tumbler and dipped the glass to a plate, then added fresh ice and poured the contents through a strainer. Kell's pleasure at the finished product showed in the gleam in her eyes as she set the drink on a napkin and smiled.

"There you go. One smokey drink." Hands on hips, she stood waiting for me to take a drink.

I leaned close and inhaled. The hint of cinnamon was there, and so was the lime. The cloudy, muted yellow color wasn't much help. I brought it closer, wanting to sharpen my sense of smell before it hit my lips. I emptied my lungs, closed my eyes, and slowly took in a full, deep breath. Tequila. Not the cheap stuff either. This drink was refined. When I opened my eyes to find Kell staring in anticipation, I sat back, content to wait for my food before tasting the concoction. Kell's hands dropped to her sides and her mouth opened. The kitchen bell dinged. She threw her hands in the air and turned on her heel. Patience was the sign of a masterful Dom, and I'd been one long enough to be content knowing the anticipation was likely driving Kell a little crazy. Whether she was aware of it or not, that would heighten her own senses and the payoff was a new appreciation for not being the one in charge. It might have been her bar, her drink choice, and her skill that made it, but it was my choice to drink it…or not. She rounded the corner and set the dish down a little harder than necessary.

"Are you going to drink it or not?"

I unrolled the napkin, placed the silverware in the pattern I preferred, then draped the material over my lap. "I'll pay for it whether I drink it or not."

Kell's eyes narrowed. "Do you want something different?"

"Why would I want something else when I haven't tasted this one?"

"God, you're infuriating."

"And you're impatient," I said as I cut one rice ball into quarters. "Why do you have such a need to control things?" Her mouth opened and closed. She'd been stunned into silence by my directness before she found her voice.

"I don't have to control anything," she said indignantly.

I chewed one of the cut bites. The creamy center and the crunchy exterior were a perfect combination for my palate. "Really?" I asked. "That's not the vibe you give off at all." I picked up the tumbler, wrapped my lips over the cinnamon sugar, and was hit by spice before the smoky, tart flavors of the beverage coated my tongue. It was sharp and smooth at the same time. It was interesting and delightful. I set it down and made eye contact. "It's wonderful. Thank you." Silence ensued. Kell stared at me for a long stretch as I slowly ate and sipped, enjoying the quiet between us. In the vanilla world it was a nice change, but I liked the soft moans that would come from being buried inside her, or the sharp gasps Kell would make as my hand slapped her flesh.

Kell came closer. "What did you mean by the note you left?"

I set the utensils down and wiped my mouth with the napkin. I'd hoped she would ask at some point, and I was ready. "You will have to share yourself with me in order to trust me." Her gaze flicked from my eyes to my mouth and back again.

"I don't usually trust people even if I know them."

"Why?"

Kell looked uncomfortable. "Because it takes vulnerability to trust."

That type of fear stemmed from a deep pain. The kind that forced a person like Kell to take control of situations in order to keep her world on even ground. It was also the kind of pain that she longed to let go of, though she didn't know how. "How will you learn to trust me if you don't show your underbelly?"

"You'll judge me."

"I could, but what if I don't?" I could see her mind working, her eyes flicking in different directions, playing out the possibilities I set in motion, though I had to question why Kell? Why was I about to do something so uncharacteristic that I hesitated. Something else I hadn't done since I was a teenager. "Go out with me. Let me show you a world where no one is judged." I thought she was going to say yes, then the front door opened, and a small group of mid-thirties flowed in, all smiles and laughter as they came toward the bar. I'd settled at the Hole because of the wide and varied age of the patrons from early twenties to sage eighties. People who hadn't seen enough but would in time, learn that they were past the age of naivety. Others who had seen too much to be shocked by anything.

When I turned, Kell was focused on the trio. Her cheeks were pink. I went back to sipping my cocktail, wanting to remember each nuance of the flavor. Taste was often an underutilized sense and I worked on sharpening mine whenever I could.

Once the group had their beers, Kell stood a little ways away from me. I finished my drink and waited.

"Do you want another?" she asked as she looked anywhere but at me.

"No."

"I'll ring your bill." She whipped around, punched keys at the cash register, then produced a slip of paper similar to the one I'd written a note on last week. Was it only last week? It felt much longer. She placed it on the bar as she picked up the glass. "Whenever you're ready."

"Are you trying to get rid of me?"

"No, I…I'm being attentive." Kell's face told a different story. A mixture of annoyed and curious. It was something I wanted to see more of.

"What's your answer?"

Kell's head tilted, and her eyes narrowed. "To what?"

"Accepting my invitation." I pulled my credit card from my pocket, along with a twenty-dollar bill.

Kell's cheeks turned a darker shade. "I don't think I should." The hesitation in her voice was contrary to her words. She wanted to go, but she also wanted me to beg.

I stood. "Have a good evening, Kell." I held her shocked gaze for a moment and left. Every fiber of my being wanted to look back. I wanted to give her another chance to answer differently, and it was so much out of how I handled a submissive

I almost did just that. I didn't believe Kell wanted me to. She was used to getting her way in her day-to-day dealings with people in her life, but I wasn't one of them. She couldn't control how I responded. The more space between us, the more settled I felt.

I slid onto the soft leather of the driver's seat and glanced at the small, but serviceable backpack that I took everywhere. It wasn't as well equipped as the duffel, but it held a fun assortment of toys, and I was in the mood for some fun, though I had to admit to wishing Kell were along this time, if only to observe.

As I drove to the private club, my mind wandered, thinking that Kell's personality type was either topping from the bottom, a manner of manipulation that a true Dominant would readily recognize, or she was used to getting what she wanted by being coy. Either tactic was useful in everyday life, but that would not work in my preferred world. While many claimed to live the lifestyle twenty-four/seven, unless you didn't need to interact with the general population at all, it wasn't an obtainable reality. A pleasant fantasy for sure, but not sustainable in real life. Even I wasn't capable of pulling it off, though I managed being content with a 40/60 ratio, with the lower number mainly consisting of my work life. The rest was for my pleasure, and I gleaned as much as I could out of it. The one thing that was missing was a full-time submissive to share it with.

CHAPTER SIX

Anger and disappointment warred inside me. This was the second time Taylor had unceremoniously walked away when I hesitated to act on a pointed question. As if that wasn't bad enough, I was pissed that I hadn't been able to steer the situation into a more familiar one for me. One where I did the questioning and was in full control. The master negotiator and problem solver. That's what had thrown me off kilter. I froze. Unable to do a damn thing except blush. *Oh God.* Had Taylor noticed?

Ha. Like she'd ever *not* notice. She was observant to the point of discomfort. Her gaze like a laser in the dark, zeroing in on me and knowing—surmising—what I was thinking. Not that she was that far off, which was also concerning. A jolt of pleasure shot through me. Why Taylor, who was both insufferable and intriguing, caused such visceral reactions left me dumbfounded.

She was still a virtual stranger. I knew more about Jack and his wife and their dysfunctional relationship than I did about Taylor, so why I cared as much as I did about what her opinion was of me, made me uncomfortable. On the heels of my discomfort was another emotion I rarely gave any consideration to. The attraction wasn't unwelcome, but she was more of a mystery I wanted to unravel. Taylor fit the bill. The strength of her aura was undeniable, and I imagined that even if I didn't know we were in the same room, I would feel her presence. Taylor was, indeed, extraordinary. A woman the likes of whom I had never met before.

"Hey, sweetheart, can I get another beer?" The man at the end of the bar with grizzled features and a straggly appearance lightly tapped his glass on the smooth surface. He wasn't someone I would call a regular, but I'd seen him a few times in the two months I'd worked here. He sat a few seats away from Jack.

Jack sat a bit taller in response and gave the guy a sideways glance. Jack had been my first customer the night I started working at the Hole. He hadn't said much beyond our general chatter at first, but the friendship was instantaneous, and I knew he watched out for me. Later I learned that retirement age was on the horizon, and I was glad for him. Aside from the cook who left at eleven weeknights and one in the morning on the weekend, I worked alone. I'd never been afraid, and I wasn't about to start now.

"Coming right up." I pulled a clean glass from the stacks and poured from the tap, tipping the glass just so. The result was a nice one-inch head of foam. I slid it in front of the man, removed the empty, and took the ten he'd placed next to it, all the while ignoring the predatory stare. It didn't make my heart race like when Taylor stared at me. This made my stomach churn unpleasantly. The five-fifty charged for a pint was reasonable. I returned his change, smiled, then moved down the bar to Jack.

"You ready for another?" I could tell he was upset, and I wanted to reassure him.

Jack glanced at the other man and they made eye contact. "As long as I'm sitting here I may as well."

I put my hand over his and gave a quick squeeze. "It's okay. You don't have to stay." I slid my hand away and waited. I was touched by his chivalry.

"It's not a hardship." His gaze softened but his smile was tight. Jack was a regular. He knew all the frequent patrons. Obviously, the guy who was currently looking me up and down was not well-liked. Jack caught his leer and stiffened.

There wasn't any reason for an altercation. I'd gotten enough of those kind of looks from men to ignore them, and unless it went further than just looking, there wasn't any need to engage. I took Jack's empty tumbler then grabbed a clean one. "Any vacations on the horizon?" He had a pretty sedate life with the exception of the two vacations he took every year. Last I knew he was throwing around a couple of ideas. His wife sometimes joined him, but he wasn't against going alone. I had the feeling Jack enjoyed the "What happens in Vegas, stays in Vegas" mentality and, from what he'd told me about his home life, I couldn't blame him.

Jack perked up. "I managed to find an affordable cabin in the Adirondacks. A week of fishing and hiking will be a nice reset." Jack worked in a cubicle in some high-rise downtown. He hadn't shared exactly what he did, but I had the feeling it was either law enforcement or some other occupation that he couldn't give details about. That was fine by me. His wife didn't share his leisure interests and I got the feeling that was okay with him. Mostly. His son, Jack Junior, had finished his degree and moved to the West Coast. I wasn't sure if he was as okay with that.

"That sounds nice." I set his fresh drink down and slid his money back. "On the house," I whispered. He pursed his lips, then exchanged the twenty for a ten and dropped it onto the rail. The tip wasn't necessary, but I wouldn't insult him by refusing it. I nodded and smiled before mouthing a silent "Thank you."

The cooler needed restocking and I was glad to have something to keep my mind occupied. The reprieve didn't last long. What was Taylor doing right now and who was she doing it with? She was too fine to be spending every night alone. It was Friday after all. The laughter that escaped was hushed, but I stole a glance at Jack just to be sure. He was focused on the television. I had no clue which teams were playing, and I couldn't help but think about what team Taylor played for. Granted, I was pretty sure it was mine, but sometimes it was really hard to tell. She'd been flirting with me even if she was aloof and a bit standoffish. Hadn't she, or was it wishful thinking on my part? And as foolish as the idea was, knowing every detail about how she spent her nights and her days had its appeal. If I let that little detail get back to Taylor, I would never find out, and I didn't want that to happen.

❖

Fuck. Of all the cursed luck I might have, Taylor strolling in with the most controlled bit of swagger I'd ever seen made me wish I were anywhere but here. That wish lasted all of thirty seconds. All she had to do was flash that fucking killer smile of hers and I was instantly damp and shy and experiencing all the other things I never experienced with women until her. What the actual fuck was that all about?

"Good evening, Kell. What a pleasant surprise."

Too bad she was so well-behaved that I had no reason to tell her to leave. If I did, she would go, and that was the last thought I wanted rolling around in my head. Sometimes those random impulses actually made it out of my mouth and tonight was destined to be one of them if I let it.

My day had pretty much sucked. The resort had thrown as much shit my way as it could, and my car needed a new battery. I'd gotten it jumped, but there was no guarantee it would start at quitting time. Since I was the closer, I'd have to play the hand that was dealt. There were worse things than ordering a ride share.

"Taylor." I nodded and stifled the urge to call her on the disappearing act she'd pulled two nights ago. "What are your choices tonight?" I slid a food menu and a specialty drink list in front of her knowing she wouldn't look at either. One perfectly shaped yet definitely masculine brow rose, making me regret what felt like a display of insubordination though I didn't know why since she wasn't my boss.

"I'm not sure why you pretend to be so strong-willed when you're clearly looking for a way to be the opposite, but I'll play along. For now." Taylor pushed the menus back.

I replayed every word, not wanting to forget anything of consequence because everything she said was of consequence. I was beginning to see that.

"Eighteen-year Macallan, rocks. An order of roasted brussels sprouts, please."

"Sprouts to stay," I said loud enough for Maggie to hear. The ice clinking in the tumbler sounded too loud for the space. Like a bowling ball striking the pins, the momentary sound was deafening. I found the bottle after scanning a dozen others. The jigger shook in my hand before I willed it to stop and ended up with a decent pour. The waiting coaster gave me an excuse to not look at Taylor before it was delivered. "Anything else?" It was ridiculous to keep talking in clipped sentences, but I didn't trust I wouldn't go off on her for acting like she didn't owe me an explanation for her abrupt departure.

Taylor's gaze locked with mine. "An answer."

It took a while for my addled brain to sort the puzzle. When it did, my previous response of anger was missing, and before I knew what was happening my mouth opened. "Yes."

"Good." Taylor sipped but didn't say anything else. The silence between us was broken by Maggie calling out.

"Sprouts are up."

I blinked several times. What had I done? Taylor continued watching me, relaxed and sipping her drink. Her eyes were hot coals in a haze of blue, a focused pinpoint in a cloudless sky. It was one of the first features I'd admired about her. In a daze, I ducked into the kitchen where Maggie took one look at my face and stopped flipping the burger on the griddle.

"What's wrong?"

How would I explain the frenzied state of my mind was the direct result of Taylor's quiet confidence and my inability to ignore her. "Nothing."

"Why don't I believe you?"

I patted her shoulder. "I'm fine." Despite the mixed feelings I *was* fine and wanted to see what Taylor had in store next, because she'd left me hanging without any details about our upcoming date. I wasn't even sure it was an actual date. Everything to do with Taylor was a contradiction.

In the short time I'd been gone, a party of four had taken one of the corner tables. After setting the plate down for Taylor, two of the group came over. "What can I get you?"

"A Stella, two red wines, and whatever stout you have on tap." The guy who did the ordering smiled.

"Menus?" I asked as I grabbed a Stella from the cooler and pried off the cap in one continuous movement.

The other guy, a little taller and handsome by anyone's standard, nodded. "Sure." He looked at Taylor who had been watching the whole time.

I didn't have to look to know. I felt her eyes on me, my skin tingling under their heat.

"What do you recommend?" he asked.

Taylor set her fork down. "Depends on what you're in the mood for." She waited a beat. "I'd wager you're a burger person. The Hole in One is a good choice." Her gaze traveled to his companion. "You're more of a wing connoisseur and would like the moonshine ones." Then she glanced at the two women they'd come in with. "A cobb salad for the blond woman, and…" She studied the redhead before continuing. "Her friend would like the lobster mac and cheese, but I'm not sure she wants that tonight. Perhaps a turkey triple-decker with fries." She smiled. "Whatever you decide, you won't be disappointed." Taylor picked up her fork and resumed eating.

I'm not sure who was more impressed by her response. I rattled off the list of reds and each chose one. The younger man paid the tab, and they glanced at Taylor again before taking their drinks to the table. I turned to face her. "When is this date happening?" My irritation came through and I hated that she could stir such disturbing emotions so quickly, but that was my fascination with her, too.

Taylor wiped her generous mouth and full lips. "I never said it was a date."

More of her condescending attitude wasn't helping. I leaned into her space and dropped my volume to a low growl. "Why are you such a dick?"

"Because you're in denial about what you really want from me."

I straightened. "Oh? And what would that be Miss Know-it-all?" I fought for control against my rage at her assumptions. They hit the mark, but I wasn't about to tell her that. She didn't need an ego boost.

Her fingers twitched, but she didn't move. "The one thing no one has ever taken from you. Control."

My breath stopped and my vision blurred. Beyond any reasonable explanation, Taylor had somehow reached inside and found my vulnerable place. The one I hid from everyone, including Brenda. Maybe Brenda had known she was incapable of giving me what I wanted and was content to let me run the show. That had been her downfall, and mine, too.

"What time do you get off tonight?" She finished the rest of her drink, and I knew she was going to leave with or without an answer.

"Midnight." The word came out as a squeak.

"I'll be back." Taylor placed two twenties on the bar, stood, then walked over to the table of four. She said a few words before they all laughed, her back to me, and I wished I could see her face before I cleared her place and wondered what I'd gotten myself into. No matter what else happened tonight, there was one thing of which I was sure. Nothing Taylor did would catch me off guard again. She was in it for the shock value. That much was clear. I had her number. Problem was she had mine, too.

CHAPTER SEVEN

A re you having a good time?" I asked the group who were obvious friends, their laughter drowning out the quieter interludes of muted conversations and background music.

"We are." The older of the two men rose and held out his hand. "I'm Rob."

"Taylor." I returned the friendly shake.

"We were just about to order some food. Care to join us?" Rob asked. The man who'd asked for recommendations was a bit more guarded. I pictured him bent over a bolster while I pegged him as he moaned in delight.

"Kind of you to ask, but I was just leaving. Who's the designated driver?"

"Lyft." They spoke in unison.

I pulled a hundred dollars from my pocket and slid it onto the table. "Enjoy your evening." I leaned closer to be heard over the uptick in volume from the piped in music. "I stand firm on my recommendations." I smiled and turned, but one of the women grasped my wrist as she stood, and I tensed.

"Wait." Curiosity reflected in her eyes. "Are you sure you won't join us?"

Her grip relaxed and I slid my arm away. She was younger than her friends, but her vibe was that of an older soul. "And you are?"

"Cassie," she said, then gestured at her companions and introduced the other couple. "Thank you for treating us to dinner."

"You're very welcome." From the corner of my eye, I saw Kell watching. Was she a voyeur at heart? Or was she fixated on what tonight might bring when she gave up autonomy in lieu of adventure? I'd wager on the second if I were a gambler, but people were more important than a silly betting whim. Kell was important. How much only time would tell.

❖

At eleven fifty-five, I stood outside the Hole. The scene my play partner and I had engaged in lingered in the back of my mind like a movie enjoyed, a pleasant interlude but not particularly memorable. That was good. I didn't want it to invade what lay ahead with Kell. The plan I'd formulated wasn't over-the-top, however, I hoped it would whet her appetite for more. Often there was a fine line between attraction and repulsion. Kell gave off a bit of the "uptight" vibration though I believed it had more to do with wanting to appear in control than anything else. The bar door opened.

"Do you want to come in while I finish? There's one customer and I'm going to lock the door."

I didn't want to be the one waiting, but I also didn't want to stand outside like a stalker ready to make my move. "Thank you." I brushed past her, not actually touching. I'd always had a hard time remembering there weren't rules about such things outside of the lifestyle and believed there should be. Too many took advantage of invading personal space without permission. I viewed it as a common courtesy that everyone should adhere to. Kell locked the door behind me and went behind the bar. A lone man sat nursing the last of his drink. He nodded in my direction. "Evening," he said.

His name was Jack. A fixture in the establishment as much as the mirror behind the bar was. I'd seen him here a lot. "Good evening." I sat in the usual spot.

"Do you want anything to drink?" Kell was draining the water from the sinks and wiping surfaces. She kept a very tidy area and I appreciated that about her.

"No, thank you." Jack eyed me again.

"Taylor and I are…" Kell paused and glanced at me with a nervous smile. "We're going to grab a bite to eat."

He gave me the once-over, then stood. "I guess I'll be going then." He was tall and lanky, and likely had the sinewy kind of strength that people often failed to recognize. I tried not to miss those type of details. I'd left three hours ago, and Jack had been here then.

"Night, Jack. See you next time." Kell continued to move around with quick efficiency. Jack nodded as he walked by. "Would you mind locking the door after Jack?"

I was grateful Jack was around a lot. Bartending wasn't easy and customers could be nasty sometimes. Kell shouldn't have to deal with that. I didn't doubt she could take care of herself, but there were people who wouldn't think twice about getting physical. I'd seen Jack's hackles rise before. "Night," I said as I closed the door then turned the key.

"Sorry about Jack hanging around. I made the mistake of telling him I needed a new battery, and he wasn't leaving until he made sure I had a ride. I've just got to count the money and drop it." Kell removed the cash drawer and set it low, so that it was hidden from anyone looking in.

"You don't have to take it to the bank?"

Kell held up a finger as she counted off a stack of twenties, then jotted something down. "No. The owner picks up the bag in the morning, recounts it, then takes it to the bank. He deposits all except the dollars and quarters we need for the next day." She continued counting each denomination, then the coins. The repeat count was quicker. She initialed the paper, shoved it in the bag with the money, and dropped it down a narrow chute. "There's a safe in the basement connected to this."

I liked how cautious and considerate the owner was. We knew each other, as much as a customer and proprietor could, and I'd always admired his easygoing demeanor. It didn't fit me, but for the people who worked for him, it was perfect. "Anything else?"

Kell shrugged into a light denim jacket and tossed a cross-body over her shoulder. "Just pulling the gate closed."

The Hole was in a good neighborhood, but it didn't hurt to be vigilant. The plate glass windows would cost a small fortune to replace and were a vulnerable entry point for someone persistent about getting in. Kell was efficient in her routine. She'd make an excellent submissive if true freedom was what she sought. Just because that was the impression I got didn't make it so, but if she let me help her explore what lay hidden she might be relieved to find an outlet for herself. She stood by me waiting for my lead and I was comfortable in letting her find her place. When her discomfort led to curiosity, I stepped in. "My car is there." I pointed to the four-door black Jeep Wrangler. It was my play vehicle. I had a boring sedan for work. It was comfy and a little flashy, but not representative of me. I held the passenger door open. Kell softly thanked me and slid onto the seat.

"Have you ever been to a munch?" With the car in gear, I pulled from the curb. Traffic would be minimal. Too late for the dinner crowds and too early for the post-event partiers. Where we were going didn't fit into either category.

"A munch?" Kell shook her head. "So we *are* going to eat?"

A chuckle escaped and I smiled. "No. We can eat later if you're hungry." How was I going to explain our destination without alarming Kell? "It's a kind of leather club for a variety of genders. It's interesting and fun to watch people being themselves." The description came out better than I'd hoped for.

"Are you a member?"

"Yes. I belong to a number of other clubs, too." I didn't normally hesitate, but with Kell everything felt different, though I wasn't sure why.

"I've been to a bikers' bar, but I'm sure that's not the same thing," Kell said as she ran her hand over the baby-soft leather that cost me a small fortune.

The silence inside as we drove through the city crackled with electricity, and I wondered if Kell felt it, too. Did she come with me tonight because she was a little curious about me or was she simply going out with a woman she *thought* was a lesbian but didn't know for sure. Hell, I didn't know her sexual orientation either and just because she was here now didn't mean there'd be another time. I wanted there to be another. We might never be play partners, but that wouldn't stop me from introducing her to the world of kink and fetishes. Being free from the confines of society's expectations and being able to live a life that was not only authentic but open to all the possibilities the world could offer was damn near perfect in my opinion. Everyone deserved to be whomever they wanted to be whether gay, straight, bi, trans, and everyone in between.

"When did you start working Fridays?" The warehouse district lay ahead of us. I cruised down the mostly empty road toward our destination.

"This week. One of the bartenders quit to pursue their dreams, so three of us are taking on extra shifts." She looked at the buildings passing by and her back stiffened.

"Won't that be a lot?" I wanted to put her at ease.

"Yes and no. I work every other Saturday for my day job, so those weeks will be a bit of a struggle, but three nights is doable, I think."

"What's your day job?" I rolled the Jeep toward a large lot between two buildings. In terms of leather and kink clubs it was still early, but there were at least a dozen other vehicles and it looked hopeful for a good showing. The thing with clubs was they ran hot and cold. One night standing room only and the next could be nearly a ghost town.

"I'm the operations manager at a resort." She snickered. "A fancy name for troubleshooter mostly."

After parking not too far from the entrance, I killed the engine and faced her. "You don't sound all that thrilled."

Kell picked a piece of lint off her pants and shrugged. I wondered if she noticed I had changed my pale oxford for a black one with the sleeves rolled a couple of times. I wouldn't be the only one to display the thick leather band around my left wrist.

"It's a decent job and I'm pretty well compensated, it's just…I'm not so sure I want to be doing this much longer. The hospitality business isn't very hospitable sometimes, you know?" She met my gaze for the first time since we got in.

"I do know. It's a lot harder than people think. Demanding clients. Being on call. Unhappy employees. You deal with them all."

Surprise flashed across Kell's face. "How do you know?"

If I were going to ask Kell to trust me, it was only right I do the same. "I'm an events coordinator. A wedding planner, among other things."

Kell groaned. "Weddings and conferences are the worst." She got out and met me in front of the jeep. Her eyes traveled over me appraisingly. "You changed clothes."

"Just my shirt." I tucked my keys into a back pocket and gestured to the building. "Shall we?" After a moment's hesitation, Kell nodded.

My natural tendency would be to place my hand at the small of her back, but I didn't have permission to touch her, and regretted not asking in advance. "Kell?" She turned. "There's one thing you need to know."

She held her little bag closer to her body. A defensive move if there ever was one. "What?"

"Don't touch anyone without their permission. Even a friendly gesture can be offensive to some of the people who come here."

"Okay." Her confusion was evident on her face, her brows knit. "Does that include you?"

I didn't want to ward her off. Her touch was something I'd been thinking about. "Yes."

Kell stepped closer. "Do I have *your* permission?"

All that was missing from the question was a formal address, but she had no way of knowing I would require one if she were my submissive. Did she even know the meaning of the term? "Yes."

Kell licked her lips. There was no mistaking the seductive sweep of her tongue. "Good." She straightened her clothes. "You have mine, too." The words were said playfully.

Clearly, she was establishing her sexual orientation with me. Heat spread from my center as I took her hand. Some of the crowd inside would be prowling for a play partner and I had to make sure if anyone approached Kell, they'd include me in the request. Boundaries were important in the world I lived in. What kind of boundaries would Kell have? Whatever they were, I wanted to be the one to find out.

CHAPTER EIGHT

I hadn't known what to expect after Taylor grasped my hand. The person at the door was muscular without being muscle-bound, his smile welcoming. The short hallway in front of us opened to a large and well-lit bar that displayed hundreds of bottles of liquor. It put the Hole's selection in a sub-par class. In the gleaming mirror, I caught the reflection of a woman who was naked to the waist and wearing a wide leather collar.

"Would you like a drink?" It was easy to tell Taylor was in her element.

"There's so much to choose from." I glanced over the length of her. For a brief instant I thought she might be packing, but when she placed her foot on the rail, the area in her crotch flattened. The disappointment was instantaneous. "What are you having?"

"Tonic with a twist." She got the bartender's attention and was greeted by an "in a minute" gesture. "I don't have more than one drink often. Too much alcohol dulls the senses."

I could go for a little dulling right now. The atmosphere was charged with dark sexual energy, but that wasn't the only energy floating around, though I didn't have a clue what it was. "Surprise me."

One of Taylor's brows rose. She leaned over the bar and spoke to the bartender, then laid money on the shiny smooth surface. "See anything that interests you?"

Heat warmed my cheeks. Taylor had a way of getting to the heart of a subject and she didn't beat around the bush when she did. There wasn't any way to hide my reaction. Playing nice was fine for work, but here, with her, it didn't interest me. I got the impression Taylor wasn't interested in pretenses either. "There's a lot to look at, that's for sure." The light, joking kind of tone I'd hoped for was missing, my nerves showing.

"Is that a yes or a no?" she asked as she set a martini glass containing a pink liquid in front of me.

"What's this?" Before I picked it up, I inhaled. A citrus scent greeted me, and my mouth watered.

"Taste it and give me your best guess." Taylor took a long drink of her bubbly beverage.

I wasn't sure I wanted to join whatever game she was playing, but I was more curious than put off, so I took a slow sip. It was tart and sweet at the same time. The lemon slice hanging over the edge was also in the contents. I tasted it again. The color helped, as did the finish. "Limoncello and Chambord."

"Very good."

The next sip, the alcohol came through, but I couldn't put my finger on it, and the inability to name it was disappointing. "There's something else in it, but I don't know what."

"It would be very hard to identify. It's Deep Eddy Lemon Vodka. A rarely used but delightfully sour liquor." Taylor leaned against the bar, not bothering to sit on the stool next to her. Everything about her was controlled, yet relaxed. "You still haven't answered my question."

It took a minute to remember. "The woman with the collar. Is she being punished for something?"

Taylor gave a small smile. "No. She has given herself to her Dominant and is owned by him. He is publicly pleased and proud of her submission."

My mind was a whirlwind of conflicting emotions. On the one hand I was appalled by anyone being led around on a leash like a prized pet, yet there was another part of me that wondered what giving total control to someone might be like? Would there ever be anyone in my life that I would be willing to give myself to them? How would it fit into my everyday life? I followed the pair as they moved among the growing numbers. His confidence was obvious, but the woman fascinated me. She moved in such a way to convey her place at his side, eyes cast down, but she didn't appear to be intimidated. In fact, she looked very comfortable in her role. I had a million questions. "Are they married?"

"I don't know them well enough to say. I know they are in a dynamic."

It wasn't the first time I'd heard the term, though I believed it was part of the BDSM scene. "I thought this was a leather bar?" Tension settled in my shoulders. I wasn't sure what Taylor had planned for the evening, but she needed to know I wasn't into *that* kind of a relationship. Even as I asked, another thought surfaced. The one where I trusted Taylor to not push me to engage in anything I wasn't willing to.

"It is. It also happens to welcome those in the BDSM world as their members."

The words played over in my head. If what she said was true, and I had no reason to think otherwise, Taylor was involved in the community she spoke of. My pulse sped up and I squeezed my legs against the surge of heat. Why was my body reacting so intensely to the idea that Taylor wanted to share a part of her world with me?

"Are you all right?" Taylor's gaze was fixed on mine when I turned in her direction. Concern creased her forehead.

"I'm not sure." I felt lightheaded, but I didn't want to go anywhere. Taylor pressed a glass of water into my hand and urged me to drink. It was ice cold and helped settle the dizziness. I took a few more sips and gave a tentative smile. "Thank you. I'm better now."

Taylor waited a beat before nodding. "Do you want to leave?"

Did I? "No. I want you to tell me more." She was about to say something when a buxom blonde in some kind of a leather halter that left nothing to the imagination stopped a few feet away.

"Dark Heat, it's been a while since I've seen you here. How have you been?"

"Hello, Mystic. I'm good." Taylor glanced around. "Are you here alone?"

"My Dom is out of town for an extended period and gave me permission to have some fun." She leaned in but didn't touch Taylor and I remembered her warning from earlier. "I've been such a good girl."

Laughter, soft yet unrestrained, came from Taylor.

"You must have been if you're out on your own."

Mystic's cheeks colored. "Well, not on my own. Kink in Kind escorted me to make sure I didn't get into too much trouble." She shrugged. "But I have permission to play if it would please you."

Taylor slid her hand onto my thigh. "Thank you for the offer. Perhaps another time."

Mystic looked disappointed. "As you wish." She turned to me. "You're pretty," she said before she walked away.

I looked down at Taylor's hand where it rested high on my thigh. The warmth of her touch sent tendrils of mixed signals from my brain to my body. Or was it the other way around? I searched for Mystic. A young, dark-haired man wearing black jeans and heavy boots met her partway across the room. They exchanged words before she lowered her head and headed down a dim hallway. He nodded to Taylor who did the same. The exchange was brief but felt formal. Or maybe I had the intention behind it all wrong and it was nothing more than a greeting.

"What was that all about?"

After signaling to the bartender, Taylor glanced behind her. She handed me a fresh cocktail and picked up her glass, then she took my hand and led me to a high-top against the wall near the hallway where Mystic had gone. I felt her watching me as I moved the swizzle stick around. Taylor's energy was palpable no matter the setting.

"You asked about Mystic. She is a submissive whose Dominant is away on business a lot. If she's been obedient and followed the rules, he will sometimes give her permission to seek a scene or a play partner. Kink in Kind is here for her protection." She grinned. "But also because Mystic has been known to take liberty with any type of permission. He will see she doesn't do more than play."

Once more, I found myself confused and aroused. "So she is controlled by someone who isn't here?" Taylor nodded confirmation. "How can anyone let someone boss them around like that?"

Taylor leaned in to be heard over the sudden volume surge in music. "In a dynamic, there's a power exchange. The submissive agrees to behave and obey according to her Dominant's rules, and in turn he cares for her in every aspect of her life. She doesn't have to worry about making decisions regarding her lifestyle under the terms in their agreement, though sometimes that includes everyday life, too."

I let it sink in for a minute as I nursed my drink. Life without decisions. What would that look like? How would it feel to wake up and know my day was already planned? That all I had to do was follow it? "But isn't that more like a servant than a partner?"

"All submissives serve their Dominant in some way, but there are different levels, and every Dominant has their own needs and desires. That's why there's a contract."

"So it's an arrangement between consenting adults?" I studied her as Taylor clasped her hands in front of her. The look on her face revealed she was considering how to respond, and I wanted to hear her thoughts about the idea of a relationship based on a piece of paper.

"Every relationship is a dynamic, whether there's kink involved or vanilla. When it comes to the BDSM community it's more intentional than the haphazard, come-what-may relationships that are considered normal. Friends with benefits are one type of a dynamic where both parties agree to not entertain feelings beyond the kink they both enjoy." Taylor sat back and the intensity of her gaze made me squirm. "It's a little overwhelming, I know."

This was a perfect segue and I jumped on it. "You're part of the community, aren't you?"

"Yes." Taylor leaned forward. "Is that a problem?"

Was it? I hadn't known what Taylor had in mind when I agreed to go out with her, but going to a kink club disguised as a leather bar was probably the last thing I'd have guessed. The whole scene was new and confusing on so many levels, but it was also fascinating. Taylor's expression and the conviction of her words alone were enough without my having to ask, but I had to be sure. Why that mattered so much was a mystery that had yet to be solved. On the other hand, Taylor had been nothing but honest from the start. It was an admirable quality.

"This has certainly been the most unique date I've ever been on."

Taylor laughed. "Unique is good. Isn't it?"

I had to laugh, too. "Well, it isn't bad." I searched for what else I wanted to ask Taylor. Things I wanted to know and what was important to me. "I have a million questions. I'm not sure I want to know all the answers tonight though." I smiled. "It might put me in overload."

She closed the distance between us by covering my hand with hers. "There's no rush. I had no idea if you were into the lifestyle or not, but it's a big part of who I am and I wanted you to see that."

Then something clicked. "Is this where you come after the bar?"

"Not usually, but I either have a planned scene or I look for play partners."

"What…" I shook my head. There was too much already and taking in more info would only muddy the water through which I was already wading. "I can't think right now."

"You know you can ask me anything at any time. I'll answer as honestly as I'm able. Whenever you're ready." Taylor's thumb stroked the back of my hand.

"I appreciate that." I looked around. The crowd had grown yet people still had room to move without having to touch anyone. The bouncer at the front door got up and pulled the door lock. Apparently, the crowd was as big as it was going to get. I took a breath because I was glad to not have to be pressed up next to someone with their body parts hanging out, but I couldn't help worrying. What if there was an emergency. Taylor must have noticed my concern.

"There's a panic button behind the bar and near the front door. If an alarm is sounded, they hit the button and the bar slides back." She closed the remaining space between us. "You're safe. I won't let anything happen to you."

I studied her blue eyes. They reminded me of flying free, like a bird in the twilight sky, and I was being lifted upward for the first time. Taylor felt like freedom. "How did you know I was worried?"

"As a Dominant, it's my responsibility to be aware of those I'm with. Tonight, you are under my care." Taylor took my empty glass. "Are you ready to go?"

Taylor was thoughtful in everything she did. She might have had no great expectations, but for some reason yet to be determined, I hated the thought of disappointing her. "I think so."

She stood, then once more took my hand. Outside, I took a deep breath. It might have been the first one since we'd arrived. Then the buzz from three drinks kicked in. Did I dare to ask for a ride home? "I don't think I should drive. I can call a ride share."

"You'll do no such thing. I'll make sure you get home safely. Do you have to work tomorrow?" She guided me to the car and opened the passenger door.

I slid onto the seat. The spinning of my head settled a bit. "Not until Sunday."

Taylor got in, then pulled onto the road. "I'll bring you to pick up your car when you're ready."

"You don't have to do that."

"I know," she said. "But I'm going to." She shrugged a shoulder and glanced across the seat. "It's what I need to do."

I had the feeling it was an argument I wouldn't win. Funny, that was okay by me. In fact, everything about Taylor was okay, and that was another unexpected surprise.

CHAPTER NINE

If it had been any other woman, I'm not sure if I would have done the same thing. But Kell wasn't any woman, and neither was I.

"How did you become so...knowledgeable?" she asked.

There were very few people who knew my whole story. I needed to decide if I wanted to share with Kell. It didn't take long. "Not many my age can boast being in the lifestyle since they were eighteen. I consider myself fortunate. I'd been taken under the mentorship of a much older Dom. At the time, he was looking for a non-sexual service person. It was a paid position, and I was a broke student. He'd had dozens of submissives by then. His style was caring, demanding, and firm, but also loving and sensual. That's who I wanted to be."

Kell turned in her seat. "Is that who you are? Like him?"

"No. I'm better than him. I'm me." It was true. I was forever grateful for all he'd shown me, and I admired the collection of resources he had shared. In my time with him, I devoured everything he offered. "After him, I took what I knew and made it my own. Then I developed my version of a unique form of a Daddy Dom." I wasn't done either. I didn't think the lifestyle was finite. People grew and morphed into a deeper level of self. They became powerful in their own skin, and it formed the basis of a power exchange. The more powerful the individual, the more powerful the exchange. "I'm still learning how to be the best Dom I can be. Not only for myself, but also for my submissives." Kell was quiet for a long time. Perhaps I'd made a mistake by telling her and the thought didn't sit well with me.

"Do you have a..." Kell shook her head. "Are you in a dynamic?"

"I have play partners, but I'm not in a dynamic relationship." I'd been in several over the past few years. One lasted for a couple of years before we decided the dynamic had grown stagnant and we ended our contract. We remained friends to this day even with the thousand miles between us. We burned a copy of our contract and tossed the ashes into the river as we said our good-byes.

"Why not a dynamic?"

I hadn't changed my social status on kink sites yet, and I wasn't sure what that said about my current state of mind, but I went with it. "I'm looking for a different kind of dynamic."

"There are different kinds?"

"More than I can name." As long as Kell kept asking, I'd answer, but I had no clue where Kell lived and I was sure she would like to get there at some point. "Where do you live?"

Kell giggled. "I guess that would help." She rattled off a street that was still a few miles away. She took a deep breath and let it out slowly. "Why did you decide to tell me about your lifestyle?"

The sixty-four-thousand-dollar question hung in the air. I wasn't sure Kell would be receptive to hearing it, but she'd been open so far. "You seemed like someone who was searching for a particular kind of freedom, and the community is where a lot of people find it." I pulled into the driveway she indicated and turned off the engine. Patience was one of the first things a Dom who's worth anything learned. Mine was good, but I had a ways to go.

"Huh."

It was all she said, and my scalp tightened. Had I unwittingly offended Kell? She was already questioning things, and if I'd gotten her desire for something different wrong, she might not be able to bounce back. But I wasn't someone who took back my words. I also wasn't against an apology when it was warranted. "Huh good or bad?" I usually had more of an inkling what was going on with my dates whether vanilla or not, but Kell threw me off level ground. She pursed her lips, and I took it as a bad omen until she burst out laughing.

Kell snickered behind her hand. "I don't think it's either, but I'm not surprised you think that about me. I mean, you're not totally right or wrong. It's somewhere in between."

I'd take that. "Will you consider going out with me again?" There's not much in my life that I wanted for, but I wanted Kell to say yes.

"No."

My internal calm faltered, and I hoped she didn't notice.

"I don't have to consider anything." Kell leaned in. "I'll go with you if you promise to tell me more about that place and the people who go there."

Kell tickled my mind, not to mention what she did to the rest of me. A picture of me slamming my strap into her over and over again to ravish her holes sent my kink side into overdrive. "Plan on dinner first. Let me have your phone." She unlocked the screen and handed it over. I made a contact entry. Name, cell, and work numbers. I thought about adding my home address, but I needed to play it safe for the time being. I sent myself a text before handing it back. "Let me know what works for you."

She laid the phone on her small thigh. "I'm at the Hole on Sunday, and I work days through the week." She picked up her phone and opened the calendar. "Friday or Saturday would be best."

Last night I'd made a play date for Friday with one of my usual partners. I wouldn't beg off for Kell. That would not have been fair. "Saturday. Six thirty. I'll pick you up here." Kell tapped in her calendar. I hoped she didn't need a reminder, but life got crazy sometimes and I relied on mine daily.

"Will I see you before then?"

I tapped my index finger to her chin. "I'll be there Wednesday." I got out and walked around to her door. She slid off the seat, and when the curve of her ass caught my eye I wanted to do nasty things to her. To bring her mind the release it craved and give her body what I knew it had never experienced. How long had she been wanting something different in her life? Had she gone looking, only to find nothing from what she already knew? Vanilla and routine. Could she give herself to me the way I wanted, or was I chasing a fantasy that would disappear like a cloud of steam? Only time would tell. Patience was my key to opening the door to Kell's desires and I definitely wanted to be the one to unleash them.

Suddenly shy, Kell didn't meet my gaze until she realized I was waiting for her to do so. "Thank you for tonight."

"You're welcome." I walked her up the steps, grazing her back with my fingertips. When she turned to me, there was a longing that rose from somewhere deep inside me. The kind that could turn a person inside out if they weren't careful. She unlocked the door and stepped inside. For a brief moment I thought she was going to ask me in. I didn't want her to. I wanted her to understand those decisions would be mine alone, with or without an agreement. "Good night, Kell."

"Good night."

The hint of sadness in her voice made me second-guess my decision to not push Kell. Not yet anyway. Even I had a breaking point. The door clicked behind me, and I smiled. The evening had gone in a different direction than I'd originally planned in my mind, but it had turned positive and Kell seemed none the worse for all she'd seen. It brought the recalling of my own first night at an event, when my mentor had introduced me to a number of people who wanted to play. I'd had the good sense to say "no." Not because I didn't want to, though. I was wet and wanting, and damn if I didn't want to try what was being offered, but he'd warned me to not be hasty, and I'd found out that playing with a stranger could be a poor decision when made out of lust and nothing more.

On the way back home, I replayed the night. Kell's majestic blue eyes had gotten wide a few times, which was understandable. There was a lot to see and probably more than she wanted in some cases. Kinksters were a funny bunch, and everyone had their own brand of kink, their fetishes many or few. Though almost everyone I knew had at least forty or fifty that they enjoyed on occasion.

As I set about my nightly routine of preparing the coffee pot, setting out clothes, and checking my schedule for the next day, the urge to fuck grew stronger. The steaming shower was meant to calm, but all it did was heat up my already stimulated flesh. I got into bed, turned on the television, and found a porn site I frequented, then flipped through screens until one caught my attention. As I stroked my distended clit, the images in front of me changed. They were no longer strangers. Kell was beneath me, my strap filling her with deep, hard thrusts. Her hands bound over her head, my hand on her throat. When I came with a moan and a thrust of my hips, my eyes closed, and it was Kell who was moaning. For me.

CHAPTER TEN

J ordan, make sure the glasses are wiped and the silverware
is spotless."

"Yes, Ms. Murphy."

I checked off the fifth item on the list in the small planner
I carried around as I headed off toward the main kitchen. The
resort's events person was on a much needed and deserved
vacation, and since I was often the backup, today was my lucky
day. Leslie, the wedding coordinator from At Your Service
event planners, would arrive in the next thirty minutes, and I
wanted to be sure everything was in place before she got here.
She represented a lucrative company with a majority of wealthy
clients willing to spend a small fortune. The more events I
could help garner for the hotel, the better it was for everyone's
paycheck, including mine. Besides, it served to keep my mind
occupied until tonight when I'd see Taylor at the Hole.

After she'd brought me home, I spent hours examining my
feelings and all the ways that Taylor intrigued and excited me.
Not being forewarned about the bar scene we'd stepped into
hadn't been as off-putting as I might have imagined, and why it
came as no surprise that Taylor was in her comfort zone among
the leather clad, and the unclad, was even less astonishing.

When she told me I looked like someone who didn't want to be in control despite the instances where she'd tested that theory live and in person, for the most part she wasn't wrong. Though to be honest, the idea of anyone having complete control simultaneously frightened me and pissed me off. There'd never been anyone in my life I could confidently hand the reins over to and be sure that whatever happened, the situation would be managed.

As if all the questioning and wondering wasn't enough, I dove into the black hole of the internet searching for terms and meanings and, ultimately, the BDSM lifestyle. There was so much information to be absorbed, I forced myself to bed three hours later, hoping sleep would claim me, but it was as elusive as my feelings regarding Taylor were.

How had she so easily caught my attention? Aside from her unique look and confident demeanor, that is. I wasn't so numb that I didn't notice, but why had I been drawn to her in a way that was so different yet so powerful it was as though she'd cast a spell. Behind all the wariness telling me that I was getting in far too deep, the pull remained. Would there be a time when the magnetism between us would waver or perhaps, would it, like all my other relationships, simply wane over time leaving me once more looking for a life that I could enjoy without all the hard work that was involved? Because every person and relationship in my past had been work. The effort to maintain them, as much as I wanted to make it so, was exhausting.

The chiming of glasses being wheeled out the double-wide, paned-glass doors brought me back. I had to do a bit of shuffling for my shift to make sure I was here to oversee the wedding that was scheduled to begin at one o'clock on the veranda. Thankfully, the weather forecast included sunny skies and moderate temperatures. The cocktail reception that followed would be a wonderful, sunny event in the shade of the old oak and willow trees that had populated the lawn over the years and left to flourish.

Next up was the kitchen. The cacophony of noise assaulted me as I pushed open the swinging door. Shouts and low mumbled curses emanated from each staff member as they scrambled to fulfill the head chef's directions and demands. He was a perfectionist, even more so than I was, and he would not be happy with anything that did not meet his standards, the height of which were more than a little intimidating. Instead of the usual controlled chaos, the scene before me was on the brink of a total catastrophe.

"Chef Louis, how are you faring for today's wedding?" I glanced around and attempted to instill a serene appearance, hoping the staff would settle a bit with my presence. It wasn't likely, since Louis would be barking orders again the moment I left, but that wouldn't stop me from trying.

"Ah, Ms. Murphy. They make you work today?" Louis believed all women with a status higher than a sous chef should have weekends off. I agreed. I also liked a paycheck that allowed for occasional self-indulgence, so I suffered along with the millions of employees whose fate mirrored mine.

"A price I gladly pay to see you." I looked around and caught a few smirks from the other chefs. "Do you need anything for today?" My culinary skills weren't much, but I could chop and mix with direction.

"No, no. Everything is fine." He glanced at someone behind me. From his tone, I could only surmise he was swearing under his breath in French. He hustled over, pointed, then demonstrated before surrendering the knife. The sous chef's face turned red as she nodded understanding. I felt bad for her. In the end, she'd be grateful for Louis sharing his knowledge, but I'd bet she was questioning why she tolerated being treated like she didn't have a clue. Louis had a reputation for going through staff, sometimes at an alarming frequency, but I knew it all stemmed from his perfectionism and the resort benefited from his culinary skills. After a final shake of his head, he returned to where I waited.

"Don't be too hard on them, Louis. I'm sure you remember those early days in your own career." To his credit, he managed to look as contrite as Louis could. I fought against smiling while he laughed.

"Yes, yes."

I pressed on to complete the pre-ceremony checklist. It wasn't as though I hadn't been through this before, but it had been a while and it was made all the harder by being preoccupied by my upcoming date. Taylor mentioned dinner, but did that mean at a restaurant or someplace that the BDSM community gathered for food? I didn't really know enough about her to surmise what she thought, or felt, or wanted. So, what did she want? There wasn't any doubt that a woman of her presence, character, and looks couldn't want for much in the way of bed partners. I stumbled to a stop, nearly taking out a large potted ficus tree. Where the hell did that come from? Taylor hadn't made any sort of sexual advances, and the cryptic way she spoke was just her way, not some backdoor attempt at flirting. Wasn't it? A voice behind me startled me enough to get my shit together.

"Ms. Murphy, is everything all right?" John, one of the front desk employees, was less than five feet away staring at me.

I straightened my shoulders and took a breath, all the while hoping that getting caught daydreaming didn't show. "Hi, John. Yes, I'm fine. Just some last-minute checks for today's wedding." He didn't look like he believed me, and I couldn't blame him. I wasn't fine at all.

"Oh, yes," he said. "Their guests have managed to fill what rooms we had. Housekeeping will be in full swing tomorrow."

The notepad I held against my thigh gave me a perfect excuse to recenter as I wrote in big letters, *Call in additional staff.* I plastered a smile on my face before looking up.

"I'll make sure there's enough people to cover the rooms." It was my job to take care of any and all details that may have been overlooked by department management because a fully booked house wasn't the norm, though oversights were rare. I liked to keep it that way.

Forty-five minutes and three phone calls later, I exhaled the breath that I'd been metaphorically holding. The wedding party was in their respective lounges with photographers. The parents of the bride had given over their credit card for the security deposit of five thousand dollars, which was required for all events of more than one hundred attendees. The florist had shown, late of course, but had everything in place with a few minutes to spare before people started arriving. The alcohol was flowing. I could go for a drink myself, but that was frowned upon by human resources. If they only knew what we dealt with they might think otherwise.

Two more hours and I could leave. The idea of being trapped soured my mood. It wasn't like I didn't have enough to keep me busy, but all I wanted to do was sink into a hot tub and let the mineral crystals I often used after a long day do their magic. I slid my feet from my shoes and rubbed my aching toes. It was time for a new pair of pumps. I didn't give two shits if my calves looked better in high heels. I couldn't race around a resort this size on stilettos without breaking an ankle. I'd seen it happen and it hadn't been pretty.

Needing something to occupy my overtaxed brain, I opened the staff spreadsheet. On a second monitor I reviewed booking numbers for the next week. They were steady but left about a third of the rooms vacant. Upper crust wanted eighty percent capacity at all times, but those numbers were going to be hard to reach until the financial markets recovered. I surreptitiously played with a few stocks, but the lingo was far and above what I could decipher, so I left the investments in the hands of experts. From the latest report I received, the eighty-two thousand I'd amassed from an initial investment of five grand had dropped to close to sixty. I was told not to panic, and I didn't. Mainly because the majority of my retirement funds were in less risky markets and that suited me just fine.

I looked at the corner of my screen to discover I'd spent the last hour moving names around like LEGO bricks, seeing who fit where and who didn't within the parameters of each employee's schedule. Now all I had to do was distribute the individual department spreadsheets to the managers, who in turn would notify the staff. I shuffled papers for another twenty minutes and jumped up the minute my time was done. Not that I was anxious to leave, but I had some prepping to do before Taylor showed up at my door, and some of it had nothing to do with what I was going to wear.

CHAPTER ELEVEN

Taylor Simpson. How may I help you?" The convenience of having two numbers attached to one cell phone was a godsend at times. At others, like now, it was a pain in the ass. I'd been working on writing a new D/s contract for weeks. It wasn't an easy task and one I'd been avoiding. Play partners were fun, but the overall satisfaction of a dynamic was missing. Someday I'd meet someone who would serve most of my needs, if not all, and I was determined to be ready.

"Ms. Simpson." The voice was tentative, soft. "It's Crystal Abernathy." Sweet, but timid, she sounded like she was going to cry.

"Good evening, Ms. Abernathy." I surmised another change was coming. Her mother, the self-appointed heir to the fortune her husband had amassed, had tried more than once to put me in my place, unsuccessfully. Crystal's requests and needs were all reasonable, and thankfully, a nice break from the usual hysterics that accompanied wedding planning. "What can I do for you?"

"I've made a terrible mistake." Her voice caught in her throat.

She sounded distraught and I was hired to lighten the bride-to-be's anxiety. "I'm sure whatever it is it can be fixed. Tell me what the problem is." A sob came over the line and I sat up.

"I should have never said yes."

What? "Yes to what, Crystal?" It went against protocol to address a client by her first name, but I had the feeling she needed it.

"Marrying him." She blew her nose then cleared her throat. "I don't love him. I'm not sure if I even like him." Her voice reflected her resolve. "How much will it cost to cancel it all?"

Not prone to panic when one of the parties got cold feet, I went a different route. "It's not that simple. Are you sure you don't want to get married? A few weeks ago—"

"A few weeks ago my mother threatened to disinherit me if I didn't go through with it."

Oh. "What's changed your mind?"

"I haven't changed my mind, Ms. Simpson. I'm just not letting her run my life anymore. I never intended to marry a... man."

How long had Crystal been at war with the knowledge she was attracted to women? Had she gone along with her mother's expectation because she didn't want to lose out on her inheritance, or because she was unsure of her feelings? "I'll do my best to keep the fees to a minimum." And I would. It was still five months away from the wedding date. Not sure how much of an emotional support system she had, I could sympathize with her quandary.

"Does anyone in your family know you aren't interested in men?"

Crystal inhaled sharply, but from the sound of the breath that followed, I believed it was one of relief. Someone was actually listening to her. "It's not that I dislike men. It's the thought of having sex with one that isn't appealing."

"So no one, then?"

"No. I haven't…it's not something that's ever talked about." I heard another deep inhalation. "I'm a virgin."

I could understand the implications of a revelation of being lesbian or bi in a family that was all about social status and appearances, however this was Victoria Abernathy's only daughter and it was about time she let her mother know. Below all the bark and bravado, the fact that she loved her daughter rang through and it wasn't far-fetched to believe her love was unconditional. "Don't you think your mother should know?"

"It would devastate her."

My Dominant side, the one that handled crises and unpleasant situations and resolved them for the better, kicked in. Devastated or not, Crystal could no longer hide who she was from her family, especially when the wedding was called off. "Would you like me to be there? I could meet you wherever you feel comfortable." No one should be forced into an identity that didn't ring true to them. Kell's face flashed across my mind. Wasn't I doing much the same with her? Hadn't I taken for granted her inclination of a submissive nature without finding out if that was a role that called to her?

I'd deal with that later. At the moment, Crystal was in need of sharing her truth with the most important person in her life, and it wasn't up to me to say otherwise.

"You'd do that? Meet with me and my mother?"

"Yes. It's not easy to share that you aren't part of the mainstream population, though the lines are blurred more now than they ever have been." I gave her a minute before continuing down the path of reason. "You love your mother, right?"

"I do. She's always been there for me." She laughed a bit. "Even when I haven't wanted her to be."

"She should have the opportunity to be there for you now when you need her the most, don't you think?" I'd had a similar conversation with my mother who said she'd suspected since I was a young teenager but let me decide when and how to come out on my own terms. Discussing kink was a different topic and one she didn't understand, but loved me, nonetheless.

"What if she can't?" Crystal's tiny voice tugged at my heartstrings. Just because I was Dominant didn't mean I didn't have empathy for those suffering. A true Dominant was in tune with all of the emotions and turmoil their subs or those under consideration, were going through.

"You'll never know if you don't give her a chance." A long silence followed. Maybe Crystal didn't have the kind of fortitude it took to come out to her mother.

"All right."

We talked a bit more with me telling her Saturday night was the one appointment I couldn't change, and Crystal promised to text me with a date, time, and location. I assured her I would be there. Life wasn't meant to be faced alone. It was hard enough with caring people around, and I doubted Crystal had made friends in the community she admitted to being a part of, or at least the community she *wasn't* a part of. Maybe she was bi or heteroflexible. More likely she wanted to explore her feelings. An important part of that needed openness and would lead to her deciding, or not, what she enjoyed and with who (Or is it whom? I was never quite sure.)

I didn't make an entry in my date book, but I put a reminder in my "to-do" list so that if anyone asked it would jog my memory to respond that I may have something coming up. Aside from my date with Kell, nothing would keep me from accompanying Crystal when she talked with her mother.

❖

The reservation I'd made was at a funky, eclectic restaurant that served farm-to-table food and a menu that catered to both vegetarians and meat eaters, like most restaurants these days. I could swing either way. With food that is. Once I sat fully into my dominance there wasn't any going back, at least for me.

Walking up the path moved me into an entirely new headspace. Excitement buffeted against calm, which was my demeanor most of the time. The need to dominate Kell was on level with the desire to watch her submit…whether that be willingly remained to be seen. There'd be no forcing or coercion. Kell would need to decide if she had an interest in the BDSM lifestyle for herself. It might not even be me she chose, and if that were the case, I would celebrate that she was embracing the hidden part of herself. Being a Dominant was a lot more than control, and I couldn't help wondering if Kell knew that part. Had she searched the internet? That would be a start, but for the truth of more than one person's opinion, she would need to experience more than one. Thinking I might not be her first Dom scared the shit out of me.

The door opened and Kell greeted me with a heart-stopping smile.

"Hi," she said.

How long had it been since I rang the bell? I didn't remember. That wasn't good. "Good evening." Somehow my brain kicked in and I took a breath. It gave me an all too brief moment to let my gaze take Kell in from her expressive eyes, down a neck that would be perfect beneath my fingers, to one of the sexiest cleavages I ever remember seeing. I didn't stop there though. I couldn't. Once I made it past her enticing breasts, her waist flared into the kind of hips made for grabbing onto while I fucked her until she was a puddle. The vision ended with me watching her dripping pussy still throbbing as I pulled out.

"Taylor? Is everything okay?" Kell's expression keyed me into realizing I'd been gone in fantasy world too long, again.

"Everything is perfect." I extended my hand. "We have reservations."

Kell stepped back for the briefest instance to grab her things before sliding her hand into mine, earning points for not questioning our need to leave. I guided her to the sedan. Her low yet dressy heels clicked on the concrete until we stopped at the passenger door.

"Did you get rid of your Jeep?" she asked before sliding onto the butter-soft leather.

I leaned down as I closed the door. "Perish the thought." She laughed, I smiled. "I use this for work, but it seemed more appropriate for a date than the Jeep, though it pains me to leave them behind." In response to the tip of Kell's head, I responded. "My vehicle is gender non-conforming, like me." I rounded the car then got in. Before I turned the key, I made eye contact with Kell. "You're beautiful."

Kell blushed an exquisite shade of rose as her gaze moved away from mine. "Thank you." She was quite uncomfortable with compliments, and I filed the information away.

The only thing missing was my preferred way of being addressed as "Sir." Kell had no way of knowing that and, despite what my mind and body were craving, she hadn't identified herself as submissive. It was a topic I'd decided to bring up during dinner. I kept the laugh from escaping, not sure if Kell would consider it a discussion she wanted to have while trying to eat, but after last week's venture she must have had an idea what was going on. "You're welcome."

Thankfully, the restaurant was halfway between Kell's home and the Play Palace. That's where we were going after dinner. She'd seemed more curious than offended by what she'd witnessed at the leather kink bar, so I was going with it. The restaurant wasn't huge, and neither was the parking lot, but I managed to pull the car into a generous spot. "Wait for me to come around." I released my seat belt, got out, and walked purposefully to her door, neither hurrying nor moving slowly. Kell looked up when I opened her door.

"What are we doing?"

I glanced over the car roof. She might not know how she identified in the world of BDSM, if at all, but she wasn't afraid to ask questions. I liked that about her. When we stood toe to toe I gave her an honest answer. "I'm spending time with you to find out what draws me to you." I settled into the blue of her eyes. "And to know if you feel the same." She trembled and her eyes fluttered. Normally, I'd take this as an affirmative, but Kell was not usual at all, and I wouldn't make the mistake of telling her who she was inside, though there was a part of her that was clawing to be heard and seen. Kell was quiet. I wasn't sure if that was an encouraging or discouraging sign. I didn't have to wait long to find out.

"Do I still get to have dinner?" A mischievous smile pulled Kell's lips upward.

"Absolutely." She slid her hand in mine.

"Good." Kell looked at the entrance. "Can we go in now?"

Unable to fathom what was going on with me, I nodded and led her through the entrance. The host showed us to a table away from prying eyes. Though not totally removed from the rest of the patrons, we were out of earshot of most. After Kell was seated, I took mine. We ordered a bottle of wine and the waiter handed us each a menu. I stole glances over the one I held, wondering if the tension in my lower abdomen was from sexual arousal or anxiety. So far, the evening hadn't been anything like I thought it would be. I was unexpectedly off base. I had to get a handle on myself and examine why I was the one who was suddenly unsure of, well, anything.

"Have you been here before?"

Kell's curiosity was endearing. I glanced around at the funky, fun décor. It was the perfect start to what I hoped would be an exciting evening of revelation for Kell, and I would get to see that wide-eyed wonder. "A few times. The food is good and innovative." I took a moment to study her, her eyes sparkling as she hung on my words. My clit grew hard. I liked when a woman paid attention. "I don't know how adventurous you are, but there are a number of dishes I'd like to try."

Kell sat up, glanced down at the menu, then once more focused on me. Without breaking eye contact, she closed her menu. "I'd like to try something different, too. Would you please do the ordering?"

"Of course." I ordered a variety of items to share. She had no idea how much I wanted to control a lot of what happened between us, but food was a start. I could take it slow. Be methodical. When living the lifestyle, just like in the world outside of a dynamic, rushing into anything without due consideration could be detrimental in many ways. I'd avoid that for the both of us. An appetizer of charred brussels sprouts would arrive soon. "What do you know about the BDSM lifestyle outside of our brief conversation?"

Kell finished her wine. "After we went to the bar, I did some searching. There's a lot on the internet."

Nodding, I cautioned her. "There is, but not all of it is reliable or accurate. You can ask me anything." The appetizer arrived and more wine was poured.

"I'm not sure I know what to ask."

I scooped a helping onto her plate, then my own. "I'd have thought you'd be curious about a lot of things and your mind spinning in all sorts of directions. I certainly was when I was introduced to the lifestyle." It felt like ages ago. I'd been a wide-eyed teen and fascinated by the display of people in various stages of sex, punishment, and the energy that surrounded me. It was the closest thing I'd found to feeling completely at home. To this day, nothing called to me like the power exchange of a dynamic. Play partners were fun and sometimes good for sexual release, but they didn't compare to a true dynamic.

"I…" Kell glanced around nervously. "I am. It's new and overwhelming."

She needed to know she could refuse and that she always had a choice. "If you're uncomfortable, you can always change your mind."

"Are we going to the bar tonight?" She set her fork down.

"No. I want to introduce you to another type of kink location. If you don't want to go, you can tell me after dinner."

The waiter set down an array of dishes with serving spoons and two clean plates. "Would you like anything else?"

"Another bottle of wine, please." I'd been pacing myself and another glass wouldn't even give me a modicum of a buzz since there was a lot of food to feast on.

"Certainly. I'll be right back."

"Wow." Kell looked over all the plates.

I was glad we had a table for four. We needed the space. I'd gone a bit overboard. I wasn't someone who did anything to impress a woman, but Kell deserved to have a wide variety of things to choose from, not only when dining, but also when it came to sexual exploration and pleasure.

"It all smells wonderful."

"Please, help yourself."

Kell lifted her plate but hesitated. "Aren't you eating?"

"I am, but I want you to take your time and sample the dishes that interest you." I gave her a quick synopsis of the five

I'd chosen. She tentatively took a small portion of each before setting her plate down and waited. "Please." I waved at her food. "Go ahead."

She waited another beat before taking a small bite of the fried chickpea, bok choy, and chicken in a spicy cream sauce. While she chewed, our waiter poured from the new bottle of wine.

"Enjoy," he said. "Let me know if you need anything."

"This is fantastic, Taylor. I wasn't sure if I'd like it, but the crunch of the peas is so unexpected. It's really good." Kell moved around her plate, sampling each item.

I sipped, content to watch her reaction with each discovery. My mind took a mental journey as I imagined her reaction with each revelation of my world, where reality and fantasy were so blurred they were the same.

Kell put her fork down and her eyes met mine. "I don't want to eat alone." The shade of blue reminded me of the sky on a warm summer day. The kind with puffy white clouds and the stuff daydreams were made of. If I weren't careful, I'd get lost in them because what I really wanted was for Kell to see the real me when she looked at me, and I wanted to see her desire to please and obey. I wanted her submission more than I thought possible. It took effort to rouse from that fantasy.

"I'm glad you're enjoying it," I said as I began to fill my plate. Aromas that made my mouth water filled my nose and I was immediately ravenous. "What's your favorite so far?" I drank wine to calm myself. I was anything but calm when I imagined what that delectable mouth of hers could do. Kell chewed and swallowed, her throat moving up and down as she did so. What a lovely neck she had.

"They're all delicious. If I had to choose just one, I'd have to go with pasta with pesto and shrimp."

I nodded in assent. "It's a great combination, and the touch of cream adds to the richness." In another life, I'm sure I'd been a chef. My love of food, along with being able to detect flavors, reinforced my wanting to try new dishes. "How was work this past week?" I wasn't someone who engaged in mundane banter, but I steered the conversation to include a variety of everyday topics. Vacation destinations, a mention of family and friends. Safe topics. Ones that I used to keep my mind in the here and now. Kell deserved my full attention in the moment, not the runaway libido that seemed to be my go-to whenever I saw her. The rest of our meal went well with Kell and I engaging in a wide and varied array of topics. Sharing a meal with someone who didn't (yet) rely on me for answers was a nice break for me and the lack of pretense refreshing.

Too full for dessert, we relaxed over coffee. I pictured a slender leather collar around her neck, and my internal battle to stay on topic was lost. It was time to introduce her to the kinkier side of my life, the one that gave me personal gratification and joy. I hoped perhaps it could do the same for Kell.

Chapter Twelve

I glanced out the windshield and watched Taylor round the car to the driver's side. Sure of movement, she was not only as sexy as my long-established fantasies, but she was charming as well. Dinner had been fun and thought-provoking. A mix of the casual, everyday conversation I'd often had on a date, but this held something more. The references to where we were heading had been somewhat vague and I wasn't sure if I should be excited about the destination or freaked out. I wasn't a person who shook in their boots when facing unfamiliar circumstances. I liked to examine my surroundings and gauge the overall vibe. Like at work, I was the one who remained calm in otherwise volatile situations.

Not that being with Taylor compared to anything I'd experienced before. No. She was an enigma on so many levels. Analytical. Controlled. Forthright without being in your face. I liked that. I liked her. A shiver sliced through me, and my body trembled. I glanced across the seat to find her watching me as we sat at a light.

"Everything all right?"

Was it? Was I? "It's great. Really. Dinner was fantastic, as was the conversation." How stilted could I get? Jesus. I needed to get a grip.

Taylor pulled the car to the curb and put it in park. "But?" Taylor asked, reading me like the open book I was, and I'd produced the page for her to read.

I wanted to look away. Wanted to be the self-assured woman most people saw. But as we stared at each other, that wasn't what I wanted. Whatever Taylor was offering I wanted to find out and she should know I wasn't going to back away. "But," I said as I took a breath. "I'm not sure I'm dressed for where we're going."

Taylor shared a slow smile. "I would have told you if not." Her hand moved toward me before she stopped. "May I touch you?"

Had a woman ever asked me if I wanted to be touched before Taylor? I couldn't remember anyone, and that too, spoke volumes about who she was, and how much I needed to trust her. "Yes." She placed her hand on my thigh and the heat radiated to my skin. I wanted her touch.

"You don't have to worry about anything when you're with me." She gave a squeeze and my pulse jumped. "I'll take care of you. Understand?"

I didn't have a clue. Brenda had done little to take care of anything. Maybe part of it was my fault for being impatient while she took her sweet time when tending to a project or making an appointment or a hundred other things. Another part was knowing I *couldn't* trust her to get it done, even something as simple as filling the ice cube trays. For some reason, trust was paramount to Taylor because she mentioned it at least once whenever we talked, and I was beginning to understand how much I wanted to be able to take her at her word. "Not really, but I'm counting on you to show me."

"Good." Taylor pulled the car into the moderate traffic, and we traveled toward the edge of town.

It wasn't long before we pulled into a parking lot beside another nondescript building. "There's nothing to be afraid of, but you don't know protocol here, and I'd prefer you be comfortable, so stay with me at all times."

She didn't have to tell me twice. "You got it." I nodded just to make sure she knew I understood. Taylor led me to a small door tucked under an overhang deep in the shadows and out of the streetlights. Though everything about it should have been a bit creepy, it wasn't. Maybe because the warehouse had been recently painted and the area around it was free of trash. Or perhaps it was the two large pots out front, overflowing with lush, well-cared for plants. Taylor pulled a card from her pocket and held it to an electronic reader. The latch snicked and she smiled.

"It's good to have connections."

She held the door open, and I stepped over the threshold. There was a distinct lack of music, which was rather strange. Unlike the last bar, this place had a very different vibe. Almost electric but not foreboding, familiar, like coming home, which was unexpected. The woman sitting on the stool partway down the hallway, next to a half-door that showed racks of hangers, most unoccupied, smiled at Taylor.

"Dark Heat, welcome." The woman glanced at me and smiled again.

"Prankster." Taylor received two tickets in exchange for the cover charge and we went to the bar.

"What do you want?"

Uh...that was a loaded question, and I didn't have a clue. While a martini was tempting, I didn't think we'd be staying at the bar. I needed to have a drink I didn't have to worry about spilling. "Stella. In a bottle." Taylor ordered my beer and an iced coffee. It was curious that she drank only occasionally. Like at the bar when she never had more than one.

"This is the Play Palace. It's a place for kinksters, and those in the lifestyle, to socialize and play. The previous rules remain, but to a higher degree. No touching without permission. Don't talk to anyone on a leash or their Dominant unless they speak with me first. If you're uncomfortable at any time, please say the words, 'The dog needs walking.' We'll leave immediately." Taylor's eye color deepened. "No one will hurt you here. This is my world and most everyone knows me." She seemed to want to say more, and it was a minute before she spoke. "It's not for everyone."

I couldn't interpret some of what Taylor had said, but one thing was clear. She wasn't going to let anything happen to me, reinforcing the foundation of trust I already had for her. That didn't mean I couldn't have fun. "I don't have a dog."

Taylor's radiant smile appeared, forming on her enticing lips. "Neither do I, but it works even better when you don't. I'll know exactly what to do." She glanced at my hand, then my eyes. "Want to go exploring?"

The invitation wasn't a total surprise. Taylor had told me some of what to expect over the course of the evening. What *was* surprising was the quickening of my pulse, and the tingle that followed wasn't unpleasant. In fact, I liked how much I wanted to do just that. I slid my hand into Taylor's. "You'll keep me close, right?" I wasn't worried, but I needed to hear it again. The last thing I wanted was to be an embarrassment to Taylor by stepping in something taboo.

"Right beside you." Taylor took a step before stopping. "I should introduce you to friends, but not with your real name."

The name others called her, Dark Heat, fit Taylor's personality if not her coloring. I didn't have a clue what my name should be. "Can you suggest one?"

Taylor backed away a step, did a slow perusal of me from head to toe, then met my gaze. "Auburn Curves."

I rolled the title around in my head. It sounded sexy and I liked that Taylor thought so, otherwise why would she have chosen it? "Okay." We left the smaller room, then traveled down a well-lit hallway painted in splashes of red and white on a black background. Did that have a significance? What did it mean? How was I to maneuver through the pitfalls I would likely encounter? Taylor squeezed my hand and turned.

"I told you not to worry, and I meant it."

This was the Taylor I knew from our conversations at the Hole. The one who was mysterious, controlled, and self-assured. The one who not only expected to be taken at her word, but also demanded it. She stood close. So close the heat of her body buffeted against me. My skin warmed and I felt lightheaded. I heard footsteps on the tiles behind us, but my feet refused to move. Taylor backed me to the wall and pressed against me, leaving room for the woman who appeared to pass by. The woman mumbled, "Excuse me." My breath caught as I felt the hard length of Taylor's bulge against me. No question she was packing tonight. What would she look like wearing a strap? What color was the dildo? How would it feel inside me? Wet heat trickled between my quivering thighs. Suddenly, Taylor's weight was gone as she took several steps back. I silently whimpered.

"I'm sorry. I overstepped a boundary." She glanced down the hall the way we'd come from. "We should go."

I didn't want to go. "You didn't do anything wrong, Taylor. I don't understand why you want to go."

"I violated your trust." She looked upset. Well, as upset as someone in control could look.

Confusion wasn't an emotion I suffered from very often, though at the moment it was center stage. There was only one thing I could think of that might be the cause. Remembering the rules, I asked "May I touch you?" Now Taylor was the one who looked confused.

"Yes."

Emboldened by her permission, I moved until there were only a few inches separating us and grasped her bulge. "Are you upset because you backed me to the wall?"

"Yes."

"And because you pressed your…" I searched for the word I thought Taylor would prefer. "Cock against me?" Her pupils dilated and the color darkened.

"Yes."

"Did I push you away? Try to escape?"

Taylor's hand covered mine. "If you did, I wouldn't have moved away because that is not who I am, but *I* lost control. That's what's upsetting." She squeezed my hand around the dildo, then let go.

I didn't want to think about what being in a relationship with Taylor would look like. Not a relationship, a dynamic. How would my everyday life change? Was I really considering a relationship with her? There was a flood of information to be had on the internet, but as Taylor had cautioned, some of it would be inaccurate. The best place to get a real picture was from the source and I was going to do exactly that. "I'm still willing to go with you down there." I tipped my head toward the end of the hall. Taylor hesitated only a few seconds.

"You remember the rules?"

"Yes."

"Then let's do this, Auburn Curves."

This time when our hands joined, there was a low electrical current running between us, and I wanted to find out how much was imagined and how much was real.

CHAPTER THIRTEEN

What in the fuck was wrong with me? I prided myself on maintaining my impulses in all manner of interactions. When it came to being with Kell, it seemed my powers of reason went right out the window. Not only had I broken my own rule of invading her space, but I was also treating her as though she were *my* submissive. She'd been gracious and game, still wanting to continue. I might have been shocked by her grab of my cock if I hadn't gotten my emotions under control, but I was able to keep a steady gaze as she did so. My clit was already swollen to twice its size and the additional pressure made it surge.

If the situation wasn't so disconcerting it would have been laughable, but one of my kinks was aggressive play and my body responded. However, without a mutual agreement, it would never work. I promised to show her what play looked like and how people engaged. Aside from that, nothing was promised, to either of us.

Kell took a pull from her sweating bottle, and I watched the dew collect and drip as her throat moved up and down. I homed in and pictured her throat with my cock in it as I held her head. The vision vanished when I heard her inhale sharply. I followed her gaze to where she was staring. One woman was bent over a bench, her bare ass exposed, and her hands bound in front of her. The male, a sadist whose name I couldn't recall, smoothed a cane along the pinkened flesh before striking. The woman jumped on impact, then settled. The strikes were inconsistent in rhythm and intensity. It wasn't long before bright red lines of demarcation and bruising appeared. Kell leaned closer, her voice low.

"Why isn't he stopping?"

How could I explain the kink they were engaged in? "She asked for the punishment, and he agreed to provide it. He won't stop until he knows she's nearing her limit, though she can stop it if she's had enough."

"She'd say her safe word?"

I nodded. "She enjoys the pain/pleasure of punishment. If she needs to stop play she knows how to make it end immediately by saying her predetermined word." Kell didn't look repulsed, just confused. "You see, a lot of the misconception of BDSM is that one person has all the power and the other has none when in reality the power is exchanged. That isn't, nor should it be, the case unless that's what has been agreed to by both parties. It's all about mutual consent and respect of boundaries."

I remembered my first time at a dungeon much like this one except there was little in the way of equipment and most of it was built by practitioners. The industry had bloomed as the word spread across the globe that there was a need for suppliers of reliable, sturdy equipment. Now there were hundreds of sites all over the world from which to order furniture to assist in fulfilling fantasies.

"What happens if she says her safe word?" Kell finished her drink and set the empty on a ledge along the wall where there were several others.

"That depends on which safe word she uses."

Kell's head tipped. "There's more than one?"

"There are usually two levels. The first one is more of a warning, and it tells the Dom or whoever is exacting the punishment that they are nearing their tolerance limit. The second instantly stops all play. Care and sometimes a discussion follows, then the decision to continue or stop is agreed upon. A well-versed Dominant knows their submissive's limits and stops before crossing the submissive's ultimate threshold. The idea is to push his or her limits, but not to the point of panic or fear. That's never the goal, even for a sadist." I could see the wheels churning in Kell. She was taking everything in while she watched. The woman's ass was marked by dozens of horizontal lines. Some were deep red, the blood beneath having pooled under the skin, while others had purpled into bruising. The caning stopped two strikes later when the woman's legs began to shake uncontrollably. She'd reached her limit, even if she hadn't said so, and her Dom knew it.

I wrapped my arm around Kell's waist and lead her to the next play station where a leashed male was being pegged by his Mistress. She'd caged his dick. He was moaning in pleasure. We watched for a few minutes before moving on. Kell trembled beside me. I was not sure if the tremors were from the adrenaline of what was happening around her or because she was genuinely terrified by what she was witnessing, so I led her to a table with chairs and grabbed a couple of waters from a bucket.

"Drink some of this. You need it." I cracked the seal and handed it off. Kell took a few swallows, then gave me a look I couldn't decipher. It wouldn't be the first time I'd introduced someone to BDSM, though it had been ages since I had. Only one person had told me I had them all wrong if I thought they were into this kind of "weird shit." I hoped that wasn't true in Kell's case. "Are you okay?" I'd promised to take care of her. I kept my promises.

"It looks so intense." She glanced across the room to another woman who was being paddled and calling out the number after each strike. Her ass was a mottled watercolor of pink, red, and purple. It was lovely. Eventually, the colors would change to green and yellow around the outer edges as it faded. Still pretty, but I preferred the newly created shades.

"It's meant to be. The power exchange is intense for both participants and each person trusts the other to abide by the terms discussed prior to the scene. For novices those details are even more important than seasoned players, but they both have to be in concert about the desired outcome."

Kell drank more, taking her time, likely letting my words sink in, then she stood. "I'm ready to see more."

My clit lengthened and my primal nature soared. Both had to remain in check. While she was curious, Kell had yet to state her interest in my world. It wasn't for everyone, but for those of us who lived the lifestyle, it could be more rewarding than any vanilla relationship.

The next area was a suspension room where carabiners and other supports hung from huge rafters and crossbeams. Built to support thousands of pounds, the beams were often used by riggers as they practiced the art of shibari, a Japanese form of rope bondage. Others simply wanted to immobilize their prey. Various play items, such as sex swings, were also spread throughout the huge space. Against one wall was a pair of St. Andrew crosses. One was occupied by a submissive I knew well. Her Dom was a talented individual and she was a seasoned masochist. They were just beginning a scene, and I guided Kell to the side so as not to distract, though the woman was already focused inward and hadn't made eye contact. I stood behind Kell, my hands on her hips, and guided her ass against my thigh. "It's important to remember that the cuffed woman has asked her Dominant to excite or punish her. She trusts him to take her to the edge of her boundaries. The Dominant trusts her to understand he knows her well enough to judge when she reaches it, and if she's capable of going deeper." As the Dom approached, carrying chained nipple clamps, Kell stiffened.

"Will she be silent?"

"That's up to her. Expecting someone to be silent through pain isn't realistic, though some Dominants demand it as a sign of utter obedience."

He approached the submissive, wrapped his hand around her throat, and said in a low voice, "You are mine." I didn't hear the words as much as I knew what he would say. I'd say the same thing if I were in his place.

Kell semi-turned, her lips close enough to kiss. I could have sworn her tongue made a brief appearance. "What did he say?"

"You are mine."

Kell's gaze slowly returned to the scene as she shivered against me. I wanted to whisper my own words to her, to tell her I had her, and to make her feel safe and cared for. That's the kind of Dom I was. Some people would call me a Daddy Dom and I guess that was more accurate than not. Honestly, I wasn't much into labels. Maybe they were more important to others, but I went with how I felt, and I always felt dominant. Submissives who gave their devotion to me favored my attention, and I was a generous Dom who could afford to be.

Snap. The first strike of the crop caught my attention as I heard Kell gasp. By the fourth strike aimed at her crotch, the woman moaned. Her face displayed her pleasure, and my attention was focused on the small platform. I wasn't prepared when Kell's hand closed around my cock and squeezed. I took a deep breath. She didn't know what she was doing by teasing me. I liked it. Snap, snap. Moan. *Wait.* That moan hadn't come from the bound woman. It came from in front of me. Somewhere between my wandering mind and the scene, Kell had sunk deeper against me, my thigh snugged firmly against her crotch.

"Kell?" Snap. Squeeze. "Kell?" My voice was firm this time, and my hand closed over hers and pulled it away. Slowly, she turned to look at me, her eyes glassy and her breathing shallow. If I didn't know better, I'd say she was in sub space.

"Hmm?" It was a half-hearted response.

"It's time to go." I gripped her hips and pushed her forward, breaking the places our bodies had touched. That got her attention.

"What?" She blinked several times. "Why?"

"Because I said so." I took her hand and led her away. She looked over her shoulder once before hustling to keep up. I didn't want to let my emotions overtake reasoning. Kell did things to me that I wasn't comfortable with, and she had no way of knowing she'd stumbled upon one of my few triggers.

Once we were outside, the cool air dampened my anger. Kell must have also sobered. She pulled her hand free. "What the fuck was that all about?"

I wasn't in the mood to explain my actions, but I'd brought Kell here and I owed her one. One of many. I ran my hand over my face. "Let's get a cup of coffee and I'll try to tell you what you want to know." It sounded lame, like I didn't really want to. I didn't. Kell had asked for nothing, and I hadn't explained anything. I'd stepped in some real shit tonight. Kell waited a couple of long beats.

"Okay, but I have a lot of questions."

I smiled, more to soften the moment than because I was happy. "I'm sure you do." I knew a coffee joint that had a passable brew at this hour of the night. We got in the car, and I inserted the key. Kell's fingers wrapped around my forearm. I ignored the streak of lightning that shot through it.

"Not a public place. My place."

Being alone with Kell where she lived wasn't a great idea. None of the ideas I had regarding Kell were great. They were self-serving and Kell had a right to understand not only my motivation for the things I said and did, but to understand me on another level. Since becoming a Dominant, there'd been no one who made me question my motives or wants or actions.

"Do you need to stop for anything on the way?" Making up an excuse to delay facing a questionable decision was so out of character I didn't recognize it at first, so I kept going. As our destination neared, I questioned again the level of my sanity, if it existed at all.

CHAPTER FOURTEEN

Is there a special creamer or sweetener you want?" Kell asked.

After inhaling to quiet my inner turmoil, I was able to respond. "Whatever you have is fine." The supplies, whatever Kell had, were of no consequence. Keeping my growing need to use her body for my pleasure was demanding all my attention and that kind of restraint held no appeal. That would never do. I didn't touch women without permission, and I certainly wasn't going to fuck her without negotiating terms and boundaries, even if it was only for play. My hand trembled as I put the car in park. I glanced at Kell and smiled. It felt forced.

Not that I wasn't happy to be alone with her. I'd been having regular fantasies and acting them out with play partners, not that they appeared to notice or care. Not having a contract wasn't my preferred lifestyle, but I hadn't found anyone who possessed the majority of qualities I was looking for in a submissive. Kell got out and I hustled around the car, meeting her on the driveway. Her vivid blue eyes bored into mine.

"Do you want me to serve you out here?"

What? Oh. I was in her way. I let out a nervous laugh and inwardly cringed as I stepped to the side. "I prefer not to have to drink coffee out of cardboard unless you've changed your mind about letting me in."

She pulled keys from her tiny bag and glanced over her shoulder. "I'd prefer you be comfortable and enjoy it."

Whatever the "it" part was, I couldn't be sure. I knew what I wanted *it* to be. Was that a flirtatious kind of comment from Kell? Would I recognize one if I heard it? It had been so long since I'd been in a vanilla relationship I wasn't sure how to interpret a lot of the everyday interactions anymore. At least, not when it came to Kell. "Comfortable sounds good." What the hell was that? She had me so off kilter I sounded like a pubescent, unsure teen who didn't have the first clue how to speak to someone they were attracted to, and when it came to Kell apparently that was me, too. The door swung open and Kell stepped inside waving for me to follow her.

"Take a look around. I'm going to go change." Kell disappeared down a hallway.

I ran a hand over my face. "You've got this," I said to the empty room. I closed my eyes and took some deep breaths. Had I ever been this shaken by a woman I hadn't even kissed or fucked? Sure, she was beautiful, and her blue eyes and auburn hair was such a commanding combination I was positive she garnered a lot of attention from both sexes, but come on. Seriously? Like, how could any woman gain an upper hand as quickly and easily as Kell had.

"A penny for your thoughts."

I snapped my eyes open, startled. I hadn't heard her return and now she stood a few feet away, a curious look on her face. Heat traveled in every direction and there wasn't much I could do to stop its progression. "I…" Did I really want to play true confessions with her?

"Keep me company while I fix the coffee pot?" She turned, giving me the opportunity to avoid the subject altogether.

"Sure." That much I could do, as long as I didn't open my mouth for more than a one-word response, otherwise there was no telling what would come out, though I had a pretty good idea it wouldn't be good.

Kell was methodical, just like at the bar. Her movements sure and precise. This was a routine she'd carried out hundreds, maybe thousands, of times. She pulled mugs from the cupboard and set them on a tray, along with various sugar packets. Then she filled a small pitcher with half-and-half. Her fingers were long but not thin, her hands carried cases of beer, buckets of ice, and much more. She was capable and strong, yet everything about her was feminine. Her makeup was modest. Just enough to bring her natural beauty to the forefront. She was stunning in a dozen ways. The coffee pot beeped, and she pulled the metal carafe out to join the other items. Then she unwrapped a small plate of cookies. When she brought them to the island, I could smell the cinnamon.

"Can you please take these to the living room? I'll be right there."

Though I didn't like being directed, as I saw that as my role alone, I headed for the leather couch and placed the plate on the coffee table that was just the right height for stretching out. The butter-soft surface almost made me moan aloud. How often did I relax on my own couch other than for a few moments to recoup some energy, only to be on the move again in the blink of an eye?

Kell set the tray down, filled two mugs, then set the carafe down. She handed a mug to me, then poured a moderate amount of cream in hers before settling back against the cushions. It gave me time to fix my own and gather my meandering thoughts.

"So, about tonight." Kell sipped, then moaned. A low, guttural sound of satisfied bliss. She was definitely going to be my undoing if I didn't buck up. "Why did we leave the Play House?"

I almost snorted, which surely would have sent coffee shooting out my nose. Somehow I managed to keep that from happening, though the whole thing was clumsy and clunky as I coughed and carried on for a bit. Composure regained, I mirrored Kell's pose and sank back into the couch, letting the warm surface surround me. "It's the Play Palace. We left because you didn't ask if you could touch me."

"You don't like to be touched?" Her face was serious.

"Touching is fundamental to most humans, including me. As a Dominant, part of the respect I demand in that position is to be asked permission before anyone touches me." Inwardly, I shrugged. "If you were a submissive in service to me, you'd be expected to show deference twenty-four/seven."

Kell sipped again, the sound the only one in the room other than my racing heart. I hoped I was the only one who could hear it. If what was going on in her head was visible, I'm sure it would be a kaleidoscope of shapes and colors. "Tell me more about being submissive."

There were a dozen ways I could respond. "First, you would always address me with my required title, along with other respectful phrases."

"Such as?"

"Please tell me more about being submissive, Sir." I had to be careful. There were things only my submissive would have the privilege of knowing. "Do you understand the difference?"

"It's the same, but without the expectation that you will tell me." Kell set her empty mug down. "The first was more of a... demand?" The question in her voice meant she thought she'd figured it out but wasn't sure.

"Exactly. I don't answer to a submissive, they answer to me. It is one part of the power exchange." I'd parted ways with my last submissive because she was too much of a brat and refused to obey. Some Dominants tolerated that behavior more than others, but I wasn't one of them.

"So, a submissive has no say in the relationship?" Kell sounded pissed.

"There can't be an exchange if both parties aren't consensual with the terms of their agreement. A submissive has rights. Being submissive is not the same as being a slave. I have no interest in slaves." The idea that a slave was my property to do whatever I wanted, and the slave had little voice in what happened to them held no appeal. The likes and details of every dynamic were chosen by those involved. Just because it wasn't for me didn't mean I should sit in judgment.

"So the woman on the platform," Kell said, her gaze changing to the faraway look someone had when they were recalling a vision. "She was a submissive and chose what was happening?"

I shook my head. "She trusts her Dom to know what she needs and wants. Sometimes a submissive will be instructed to ask, but the Dominant has final decision. Whether for punishment or pleasure, he or she has the power of choosing what that is, as long as he provides what the submissive needs." A dynamic wasn't complicated. It was difficult to decipher because it fell far from what society saw as "normal" behavior. Whatever that was supposed to mean. I wasn't the type to adhere to what others dictated. "Sometimes it's an act that is meant to recenter or refocus and calm the submissive. Sometimes it's to build upon their sexual needs and heighten their desire to orgasm." Kell's movements told me she was fighting her own urges and desires. The constant fidgeting wasn't there when she worked at the bar.

"How does someone know?"

It was my turn to be confused. "Know what?"

"If they're submissive, or Dominant, or…what did you call one of the other people?"

"Some people are Switches. They like to change roles between being dominant and submissive."

Kell's eyebrows knit as she considered it. "Does that really work?"

"Some people are very good at it. They can be totally submissive one time and be dominant the next." A few of my play partners were Switches. That wouldn't work for me in an established dynamic. "Are you okay?"

"It's a lot to process."

I sat up and moved a couple of inches closer. "I made some assumptions when I brought you to the bar, and then to the Play Palace. That was wrong of me. I should have asked if you would be interested in finding out about the lifestyle."

"Why did you?" Kell's lips pursed. "Assume, I mean."

As much as I dreaded having to admit I'd jumped ahead when it came to Kell, it was time to have the conversation. "When I first saw you I couldn't help noticing how gorgeous you were and wondered what you were doing bartending. I mean, there's nothing wrong with the profession, but why at the Hole? After seeing you a half-dozen more times, I sensed something else. There was an undercurrent of unrest. Some element of you that wanted something different, something new. I wasn't sure until we talked those first couple of times what it might be, but then I recognized what I'd seen in many of those who'd stumbled into the BDSM community."

Since Kell wasn't protesting that I had been wrong in my summation, I went on. "You longed to be fulfilled in ways you'd only imagined. Wanted to be challenged in ways that spoke to your inner self…your inner sexuality. And you wanted a break from the day-to-day demands and decisions that had worn you down." I extended my hand and waited. The next move had to willingly be Kell's. When her hand slid into mine, my entire being settled. The lesson in trusting my gut from here on out was a bonus.

"I'm not sure about much these days except if I'm going to explore the part of me you're talking about, I want it to be with you." Kell's eyes sparkled with emotion.

Wanting to take her and make her mine was instinctual, a primal hunter set on taking down their prey. Another, deeper and newer type of desire wanted so much more. For the first time in my adult life, I wanted a lifetime relationship. One that would fulfill my kinky nature for certain, but also with someone to walk through life with, in every possible way. Could Kell be that person for me? And just as importantly, could I be that person for Kell? I was damned well going to find out if she had similar interests or if she was simply curious.

"The lifestyle is challenging, but also very rewarding, though it's not for everyone, Kell. I can show you my brand of it." What would be the best approach for a novice was my first consideration. "I'm going to bring you a few books to read. Nothing too intense, but they'll give you an overview of expectations, rules, and general information. After you read them we'll have a discussion and I'll answer any questions you have to the best of my ability."

Kell squeezed my hand once. "Then we go back to the Play Palace?" Her enthusiasm for more was adorable but naive.

"Maybe. There's no need to rush into anything. You need to take your time and so do I."

"Why?"

I took a deep breath. "Because I want you to be my submissive and at the moment it's a one-sided desire that won't work for either of us." I hadn't planned confessing my dark thoughts. Well, not dark as much as hidden. Kell must be thinking I was a predator of the asshole variety by now, and I couldn't blame her. The blush on her cheeks might be convincing enough to tell me otherwise.

"I'm sure you could have any woman you want." Kell attempted to pour more coffee into both our cups. The carafe shook in her hands.

"I'll pour," I said. She nodded and I took over. Her willingness only fueled my already burning desire to find out if she could give me the type of obedience I'd demand. My mind engaged in the sort of imaginings that should be reserved for the person who wore my collar. Kell sat waiting. She deserved answers. "Whether that's true or not, the number isn't what matters. It's the person and their commitment to being the best they can be for themselves and trusting me to guide them to a better and more fulfilling life."

Kell fixed her coffee, her hands steadier. "How do you know what I need, or want?"

The question was a common one. It's what every novice sub asked at some point. "Dominants have to be good observers to be effective. At least, that's how it is for me. It's how I learn what guidance and encouragement for a more fulfilling and authentic life, is needed. Or what form of punishment would be effective."

"I thought BDSM was centered around sexual needs and desires." Kell's brows were wrinkled.

"Play partners usually engage for some type of physical release. It might be sexual or some kind of kink, or what you might consider punishment, though that's not always the case. Some people experience intense pleasure from floggings or other stimulation." I wasn't sure how much more information would be helpful at this point. "A dynamic is much more than physical. It's mental and emotional, much like vanilla relationships, but with open, honest communication and clarity, as well as strict boundaries." It was clear by Kell rubbing her temple she had enough to think about for one night. "It's getting late. I should go," I said as I stood.

"Are you sure you have to leave?" Kell glanced around. "I could make more coffee or fix you a drink."

"That's awfully sweet of you, but I'm sure you could use some rest." I held her chin and smoothed my thumb over her cheek, feeling the pulse in her neck race. She leaned into my touch. If I didn't leave I would take more from her, and while she might think she was willing to do what I wanted, I doubted she was ready. I brushed my lips over the place I'd rubbed before breaking all contact.

"I suppose you're right." Kell's voice was low and shaky.

I couldn't keep from smiling. "I always am." She walked me to the door. "We'll talk more about tonight, or whatever else you want to know."

"Thank you for dinner and the lesson." Kell leaned against the open door as though she was too tired to stand.

Would she fall into bed so emotionally drained that exhaustion would overtake her, or would she focus on the scenes she'd witnessed and play with her pussy until she let out a moan of pleasure? I hoped it was the second scenario. Thinking about her playing with herself and thinking of me was another option and would fit into my own needs well. "Good night."

I let the visions follow me home where I tore off my clothes and rubbed my hard center until I was spent. On the edge of sleep and dead tired, my mind conjured Kell in my bed, her warm body pressed to mine and her head on my chest. I could get used to that vision, but the fantasy wouldn't do for long, and that was the part that both scared and excited me.

CHAPTER FIFTEEN

The sheets beneath me were cool against my feverish skin. All the while I got ready for bed, all I could think about were pieces of my conversation with Taylor. How had she recognized the gnawing, distracting unease that had plagued me since…I had no idea how long.

I'd become so confused by the myriad of emotions and physical stirrings that I barely recognized them as my own. Brenda hadn't even come close, but she hadn't ever paid much attention to the things that mattered to me, and it had been a big reason we couldn't make it work. I'm not sure I ever wanted it to. But Taylor paid attention to the things that mattered to me. The things that made a difference, or would, if I ever had an opportunity to be the kind of woman I'd only thought of becoming before Taylor.

After letting out a loud sigh that echoed against the ceiling, I flipped to my side and hugged one of the many pillows I had on the bed. They helped fill the empty space that I hoped would one day be occupied by a woman who knew and understood me, not just tolerated me. Someone who actually cared about the things that were important in my life. "*A dynamic is much more than physical.*" Taylor's words came with a sense of conviction, as though she lived and breathed them, maybe she did. Was what she said true?

An hour later, sleep still hadn't come and I threw back the covers in frustration. What the ever-loving fuck? I didn't suffer from insomnia. More like I fell into bed so exhausted I passed out. Sitting on the edge of the bed, I tried to think of something constructive to do. I wrapped myself in my favorite worn robe and headed down the hallway to the study, then turned on my computer. My throat was parched, and my stomach grumbled enough to demand attention. The kitchen was sparse in choices. Grocery shopping was rarely a priority. I usually ordered take-out or snagged something from the kitchen at work. Guests in my home were rare. I opened the refrigerator and stood staring at the nearly empty shelves; the door held a variety of condiments, dressings, and assorted jars of long-forgotten sauces. The pantry offered little more. I snagged the box of microwave popcorn and found a lone package inside. The expiration date was one I could live with, so I ripped open the wrapper and unceremoniously tossed it inside, pushed a few buttons, and waited. The water from my personal cooler was ice cold and soothing. I rarely craved water and nearly emptied a second glass as I looked out the window, seeing nothing. My mind was still a canvas of random images from last night.

The ding that announced my early morning meal was ready broke the flashing stream of pictures. Once the steaming bag was open, I poured the contents into a bowl, grabbed a paper towel, and stalked back to the waiting computer. What did I want to know? Taylor had used a few words repeatedly; starting there only made sense. I typed in the word *dynamic*. After a few random and general references, I changed tactics, *BDSM dynamic*, and the desired results flashed on the screen.

BDSM dynamic is a term for the roles consenting people adopt and the way they behave toward each other in the BDSM aspects of any relationship or scene.

Now I was getting somewhere. Each search revealed more phrases and words, and they all had a focused meaning, especially when I located a BDSM glossary of terms. One theme appeared everywhere.

Safe, sane, consensual. The words repeated like a mantra with every article I read. *It is by these three tenets that the BDSM community is said to differentiate ethical play from sexual practices that would otherwise be condemned as reckless or coercive.*

Further explaining that exploring the dynamics of dominance and submission was a huge part of sexual development only added to the unsubstantiated mystique of a lifestyle I'd only heard talk of here and there. Now I knew why. The lifestyle was as sacred to those living it as matrimony was for those who honored it.

"Huh." The word was loud in the quiet space. I continued to follow threads and ended up down so many rabbit holes, I knew this must be how Bugs Bunny felt. Squinting at the tiny clock on the screen and noting the time, I moaned. Where had the last three hours gone? It wasn't like the research was boring, but some of what I read had me questioning a lot of my societal preconceptions. Nothing I thought I knew was real. It was the stuff of movies and porn, based on half-truths and runaway imaginations. Taylor offered reality. Whether I was ready or not would have to wait.

CHAPTER SIXTEEN

I'm not sure why we're meeting at such an odd hour. I thought you said you had everything under control." Victoria Abernathy looked annoyed to say the least. Crystal sat within reach of her on the corner of the conference table and I had taken my place next to Crystal.

"Let me reassure you," I said to Victoria. "Everything is under control." When I made eye contact with Crystal, she shared a nervous, not-quite smile. I squeezed her hand and nodded.

After a deep breath, she straightened in her chair and looked at Victoria. "Mom, I can't marry, Richard."

"What do you mean? Of course, you can. He comes from a good family, is on the fast track for—"

"I don't love him. I'm not marrying someone I don't love."

Victoria reached for her daughter's hand. "Now, dear, everyone gets cold feet. Even if you don't love him right now, I'm sure after the wedding you'll see how good your life will be."

"Mom, that's not it. I don't love Richard because…well, because he's…" Crystal's earlier resolve began to crumble.

Against my earlier conviction of letting Crystal do this her own way, I couldn't sit by and watch her struggle. "Mrs. Abernathy, what Crystal is trying to tell you is that she isn't interested in marrying any man." I hesitated outing her because she needed to be able to say the words herself. It was the only way she'd withstand the onslaught of questions from friends and family.

"What are you saying?" Victoria asked me, then looked at Crystal.

"What Taylor is saying, what *I'm* saying, is that I'm not the least bit attracted to men. I'm attracted to women, Mom. I'm pretty sure I'm a lesbian."

Again, Victoria glanced between us, then at our joined hands. I didn't want her to think I seduced her daughter, so I slid my hand away.

"Is that why you're here? Because you two are a couple?"

Crystal spoke up this time. "No, Mom. Taylor's here for moral support. I've never been attracted to guys. I only dated them because I couldn't stand the thought of disappointing you, but I can't lie to myself anymore." She hung her head. "I just can't," she said, her voice barely above a whisper.

It took a few minutes of intently watching her daughter's internal struggle before Victoria reached for her. "My dearest Crystal. You're my daughter and I love you." She held her hand, touched her face, and smiled wistfully. "There's been times when I thought maybe you were looking for a person who didn't exist. You always found one excuse or another to not go on a second date, or that there was something odd about this boy or that one. Then you started dating Richard and I hoped he would live up to your expectations."

"He was the only one who seemed to understand me. Maybe not in all the ways, but at least he thought about something besides sex. We became close, but I think we both knew it wasn't going to work in the long run."

"Then why the engagement and the plan to marry?"

Crystal shook her head. I wasn't sure if she would say more, so I squeezed her hand to let her know everything would be okay. "I think we both wanted to believe we could make it work somehow, but that was a lie. We both know that now."

Victoria looked at their joined hands. "You agreed to meet with me even after I was so demanding about the wedding plans. Why?"

I slid my hand away and let my professional side take over. "Because I believe in the strength of a mother's love. I had a feeling if you knew how unhappy your daughter would be marrying someone she'd never share the kind of love people need to be happy, you'd support her decision to call off the wedding."

"And about being a lesbian?"

"For all your demands, I recognized you only wanted the best for Crystal. That you wanted her to be happy above all else." I glanced at Crystal. "I still do."

"Looks can be deceiving, Taylor. When we met, I wasn't sure if you were the right person to plan this wedding. I was wrong. You were the best person to support my daughter's vision of the future. I appreciate that, and you being here today."

"Thank you." I stood and patted Crystal's shoulder. "You two stay as long as you like. I'm going to send out emails to the vendors with the news the wedding is officially off."

An hour later, Crystal came to my office and knocked on the frame. "We're going to have a drink and a bite to eat. Care to join us?"

I went to the door. "Thank you, but no. I have a delivery I need to make."

"Are you always working?" Crystal leaned in the doorway, much more relaxed than I'd ever seen her.

"Not everything I do is work-related." I grasped her forearm. "I'm so glad everything with your mom worked out."

"I'm glad I listened to you. We still have a lot to talk about, but it's going to be nice to not have to deny my feelings anymore." Crystal pulled me in for a hug so quickly, I didn't have a chance to react. "Thank you." She let go and stepped back. "I better go before the queen has my head for keeping her waiting."

We laughed at the reference. "Don't worry about anything but solidifying your relationship with your mother. I've got things on my end."

"I know you do." Crystal disappeared down the hall.

I was warmed by the thought of helping someone embrace their true nature. Kell needed my help, too, believing she was a little lost at the moment by conflicting thoughts of what she might want versus what was acceptable. I could show her and give her answers. As much as I wanted her submission, I wanted her to be able to come to a decision about her own sexuality and desires based on fact instead of folklore.

Chapter Seventeen

Is something bothering you?" Jack asked. The beer I'd just delivered to him had a three-inch head of foam.

I grabbed the glass and dumped off most of the foam, then refilled it properly. "I'm fine. Just thinking about work." This was work. "My day job." That's what I said out loud to convince both of us that I wasn't hoping Taylor would show up for her one drink, one appetizer visit, even if I did think it highly unlikely. That's where my nerves were getting to me. I was anxious about *not* seeing her. After last night's marathon surfing the net, I'd fallen into bed exhausted, not waking until well after ten. I'd been thrown off for the whole day, fidgeting and fussing over routine tasks of laundry and housework, and arguing that what I was doing wasn't even close to what I wanted to do.

Instead of the ho-hum of everyday shit, I wanted to get lost in the world of kink. Funny, I'd picked up a dozen terms overnight and liked how they rolled off my tongue. How I wanted to use my tongue, or rather how Taylor would use my tongue and mouth for her pleasure sent electric currents through me, heightening my senses. I felt alive.

Jack, God bless him, continued to study me but remained quiet. Knowing he cared wasn't as uncomfortable as it might have once been. In the big picture, I hadn't had a lot of positive attention in the course of my life. It wasn't a complaint as much as a reflection on things I'd gone without. Lately though, the things I'd survived with not having weren't as easy to ignore. Taylor had awakened a buried need. I was so tired of being the go-to at work without having my own go-to...anywhere. Maybe *that* was what Taylor recognized because she was right about one thing. I didn't want to be in charge of my personal life any longer. A silent laugh rose. I'd made such a mess of things with Brenda, and before her it had been...? My gaze narrowed. How pathetic was it to be unable to remember the woman's name who I'd dated for almost a year until I couldn't take the bland life I was living any longer. *What the fuck was her name?*

"Kell?"

I looked up at Jack. "Hmm?"

"I think that glass is clean."

In one hand was a bar towel, my fingers holding it against the glass I held in my other. The damn thing nearly sparkled, devoid of even a trace of lint or prints. My face heated. "Thanks," I mumbled, my head down.

"I don't mean to pry, but you're definitely preoccupied, and that's not your usual style." Jack took a drink, looking into the mirrored reflection of us both. There were other people dotted throughout the bar, but no one was looking my way, except for Jack.

"It's a temporary state, Jack. No worries." He looked like he didn't believe me any more than I believed myself, especially if temporary meant not interacting with Taylor. "Honestly, it's just a thing I'm trying to wrap my head around."

The door opened and my pulse soared until I saw a middle-aged couple stroll in and take a seat at a table. "Welcome," I said from behind the rail. "What can I get you?" I wasn't supposed to wait tables, though for the occasional older or disabled person who came in I made an exception. The couple smiled and the man approached after noticing the small placard on the table that said "*Bar service only.*"

"What's on tap?"

I rattled off the current selection that included some local seasonals. The man chose an IPA and after a brief conversation with the woman, she went with the stout. "Would you like to see menus?"

The man took a drink and smiled. "I could definitely go for something." He glanced over his shoulder and the woman nodded in agreement.

"Take your time. The kitchen's open until eleven." Maggie, the cook, was single and didn't mind staying later than her scheduled time, but a job that consumed a person's life wasn't how anyone should have to live. *Huh.* That was funny coming from me. I'd lived that way the last five years until coming to the Hole for a change of pace. What hadn't been part of my plan was Taylor.

Closing down the bar turned into a disappointing end to an otherwise quiet night. Taylor hadn't shown and the disheartened feelings I had were no one's fault but my own. She'd made no promise, and maybe that was part of the anxiety I was experiencing. I wanted promises from her.

Jack had left an hour ago. I wasn't convinced he believed there wasn't more going on with me than I confessed, but I wasn't about to tell Jack about wanting Taylor to do things to me that I only thought about in the sanctity of my bedroom where no one judged or cared if I wanted to be tied down and made to endure all manner of pleasure, or maybe something I never thought I'd enjoy. What was that term for being on the brink of orgasm over and over? Shit. I really needed to write things down or get a book. I flicked off the lights, bolted the door, then pulled down the gates. The voice close by startled me to the point that I was shaking when I turned around.

"Kell."

And just like that, there was Taylor, as though all my thoughts had coalesced into some magical conjuring. My hand had flown to my chest in surprise, but with Taylor looking at me with that particular form of intensity she possessed, I felt foolish. "What are you doing here?" Maybe I should have been annoyed she'd waited till now to show.

"I was going to drop these off earlier, but I was running late for an appointment." Taylor held out a few slender books.

Anger flared inside. I didn't want to know who Taylor was with earlier, and I certainly didn't want to know what she'd been doing. "Were you at the Play Palace?" I asked and placed my curled fists on my hips.

Taylor's brow furrowed and she took a step closer. "No, but if I had you wouldn't be getting any details about it. My ethics run high. What I do with another person is personal." Taylor took another step. "Not so in control now, are you?"

I felt like a chastised child, but she was right. What she did or didn't do wasn't any of my concern. I shook my head and sighed. "I'm sorry—" I was going to apologize before Taylor's swift movement caught me off guard and I found myself backed up against the metal gate.

"You want to know what I do?" Taylor dropped the books she was holding.

I stood slack-jawed. This Taylor was feral...primal. My mind disengaged for a minute, but before I could do anything, before I had a formulated thought, Taylor's hand closed around my throat. Fear and excitement coursed through me in equal amounts. I was turned on beyond anything my wildest imagination could even conjure.

Taylor moved her head next to mine, her lips beside my ear. "First I immobilize my prey." Her voice was low and commanding. "Then," she said, "I fuck their needy cunt." Her hand was in my crotch before I registered what she was doing, her thumb zoned in on my tight clit. "Is your cunt needy, Kell?"

As much as I knew I should be scared, I was interested in seeing what happened next. To *feel* what happened next.

"Well, is it?" Taylor's fingers tightened a little more.

"Yes."

The silent stare, the primal stance, the possessiveness from Taylor made everything else fade into the background. I leaned into her touch, and she backed away.

"You don't know what I need or want, but I know what you need. I always will." She picked up the books and handed them to me. "I'll see you Wednesday."

The passage of time seemed to be inconsequential. Taylor had gone to her Jeep, watched me through the windshield until…I'm not sure what she was looking for. The second she was gone and I no longer felt the heat of her gaze, I was left cold, and wanted her singular focus again. I pushed off and looked at the books in my hand. *BDSM for Beginners. Whatever You Thought You Knew, You Don't. The Heart of Dominance.*

I hustled to my car. I had reading to do. It was going to be a late couple of nights.

CHAPTER EIGHTEEN

I rapidly walked through the offices, ignoring the "Good morning" greetings being called out. I headed directly to the break room in desperate need of another cup of strong coffee. Not sleeping well wasn't an affliction I often dealt with, but when I did it felt as though my entire body was exposed and even the air currents around me were irritating. My clit was extended and throbbing and no matter what strategy I used in an attempt to relax, nothing was working.

The object of my anxiety was Kell. When I saw her, I wanted her on her knees ready to serve me. Instead, her questions had only served to piss me off and I lashed out, touching her without permission and almost taking her down right there on the street. *For fuck's sake.* I had to shake off this pall of uncontrolled emotions. Anger in a scene could be useful to a certain degree, but in the work world it would spell disaster.

With a steaming cup of coffee, I went straight to my office. There were a couple of additional vendors I needed to cancel for the Abernathy non-wedding. No matter what was happening in the other part of my life, I still had the business to tend to. I could lament my ill-placed temper later. I no sooner settled when Les strutted in. Her immaculate, professional outfit looked ten times better than the slightly wrinkled one I wore, another visible sign that I wasn't in a good place.

"I see a client canceled," she said. She leaned a hip against my desk and stood over me. If that was her attempt to show her superiority, she'd be sorry.

"Crystal Abernathy came out to her mother and called it off."

Les gave me a stern look of indignation. "Did you make a pass at her?"

"What?" I jumped to my feet, nearly knocking over the coffee cup, and shouted at the accusation. "Are you fucking kidding me?" I'd never do anything as backhanded as try to seduce a client.

"Ouch. Have I rubbed a sore spot, or did you wake up on the wrong side of the bed?"

I rubbed my hand over my face. "Just drop it, okay?" Between not sleeping and being unable to stop thinking about the look on Kell's face when I throated her, I was literally going a little bit crazy.

Les's features softened. "Hey," she said as she came closer and put a hand on my arm. "What's going on?"

When push came to shove, Les always had my back and this situation would be no different. "I've met a woman."

"Not unusual. Go on."

"She's curious about the lifestyle and I've been introducing her to my haunts." I could try to tell myself I was doing the neighborly thing when in reality both Kell and I knew there was more to it since I'd said as much.

"This isn't the first time you've done that. In all our years of friendship I've never seen you ignore the staff or snap at me, so what aren't you telling me?"

"I want her." I dropped into my chair. This time Les took one of the seats in front of me.

"Do you mean like in wanting to date her?"

I looked directly at Les. "No. I want her as my submissive."

Les whistled low. "Wow. That's the first time I've ever heard you talk about someone outside of the lifestyle in that way. What about her is different?"

"You mean aside from being gorgeous and curious?" I knew perfectly well what Les was asking because it was the same thing I'd asked myself time and again since the first moment I saw her. "Kell *is* different." No matter what level of reasoning I used, the simple truth was that Kell was the only person I thought of when I considered what a lifetime D/s relationship could possibly mean or look like. Les continued to stare to the point I began to grow uncomfortable. One more sign Kell had me so off kilter I was questioning every decision.

"I've never seen you with a faraway look when talking about a woman before." Les moved to the end of the chair, elbows on her thighs, and a look of genuine concern firmly in place. "Tell me everything."

Les wasn't only my business partner. She was also a friend of nearly twenty years. There wasn't much I didn't tell her, except for what I considered private between me and my submissives. She knew not to ask for details in that regard. "I'm at a loss myself. Kell gave no indication she was interested in the lifestyle, but I recognized a restlessness. A kind of wanting something different, wanting more." I shook my head and tried to make sense of all the random thoughts that made their way into my conscience.

"You think she wanted to find out about your kinks?"

"No. I think she didn't have a clue what she wanted until I showed her what else the world had to offer." Physically restless,

I wriggled in my seat. "She was so curious for more, I took her to the Play Palace."

"Oh shit. Did she freak?" Les went to my mini fridge for water, then handed me one.

"Kell was mesmerized." I took a drink, then breathed deeper. "I'm the one who freaked."

Les was about to sit but froze midway. "Wait. What? You?"

"Yes, me." It was my turn to be on the move and I paced toward the window where my view was all sharp edges and angles. Glancing without really seeing, I looked downward. There, a pinpoint in the distance, a tree grew. It was vivid in the stark landscape, and then I got it. Kell was my focus point. When the lifestyle became acts without emotion, when there was no true power exchange, I went looking somewhere different. For *someone* different. "Kell moves me to act without the checks and balances I've come to rely on. She stirs feelings much deeper than I've ever allowed a woman access to, especially outside of the community."

Kell was going to be the one to save me from myself. Acting robotic wasn't who I was. It was time I went after what I wanted my life to look like. Kell was the who to help me get there. I was as certain of that as the need for air. The only problem was, Kell hadn't said she wanted to be submissive to anyone. She was curious and wanted to explore, but that didn't mean she'd be kneeling before me anytime soon, if ever. Knowing this only added to my frustration. I had to put my own urges on the back burner until I knew for certain Kell wanted to explore what I was offering, not only in general, but specifically for me.

"What's your plan then?" Les sat back, willing to give me time to answer.

Did I have a plan? What, if anything, would give me respite from the constant turmoil surrounding my feelings for Kell? I really wished I did have a plan because ignoring my volatile reaction wasn't an adult way to handle what was going on between us. I turned and smiled. "Fuck if I know."

Les gave me that one-sided grin of hers that told me no matter what I did, it would all work out, at least in Les's eyes. "Ah, the old duck and cover plan." She dropped her empty into the recycle bin and clamped her hand on my shoulder. "Sometimes it's better not to have a plan, my friend, otherwise we just fuck everything up." She gave me a hug and left me to my thoughts.

Two more days before I saw Kell again. Before then I was going to call one of my closest friends in the community. They had decades of experience and had become exclusive with their last submissive. If anyone had words of wisdom, it would be him. He'd been instrumental in showing me how to be the best Daddy Dom, notwithstanding, my degree of demanding kink.

One thing I did know, I was going to ask Kell to tell me about her last relationship and why she was single. A woman like her had so much to offer I found it hard to believe she wasn't at least dating. I huffed aloud. Maybe she was dating, and I just didn't know it because I hadn't even bothered to ask. I was so wrapped up in what I wanted, I forgot my obligation to honor boundaries. What a shit move that was.

Not to ignore the obvious, but after that little show I put on the other night, it was a wonder Kell hadn't blocked me. Oh fuck. Had she? I wouldn't know unless I tried to call or text her, and I hadn't. But I should. Maybe apologize for the way I acted. I wasn't sorry for what happened, and I wasn't going to ask for forgiveness either, but I did owe her an apology for not asking if she was okay or wanted to talk about it before Wednesday.

I took a breath. If Kell didn't answer or didn't want to talk to me, I'd make a point to keep trying. The possibility of not exploring more with Kell wasn't an outcome I was willing to accept.

❖

My head throbbed and my stomach did an unpleasant slow roll. The last of the vendors from the Abernathys' were sympathetic, but without revealing the real reason the wedding had been called off, the florist was still going to charge twenty percent of the total order. I'd done my best, but according to the invoice that Victoria signed, a minimum of six months cancellation notice was required or they could collect the entire amount. Twenty percent was a generous concession, even if I was just shy of the minimum by three days. We threw a lot of business their way, but neither of us would win if we pushed too hard. Victoria assured me she'd gladly pay for her daughter's happiness.

"Mrs. Abernathy, it's Taylor."

"Taylor, I didn't expect to hear from you for at least a few more days."

I sank into the soft leather and took a second to enjoy the comfort of the softness. I wasn't all hard edges and planes. Kell provided relief from the hard edges, too. My hope was that Crystal had found some relief for her anguish in her mother. She was lucky to have such a smart woman on her side. "I've taken care of canceling the florist and the band." The numbers on the pad in front of me were still sizable. "The best I could do was twenty percent of the total for each. That's just shy of ten thousand."

"It's fine. Honestly, I thought it might be the entire bill for both of them." Victoria paused. "What did you tell them as to the reason?"

I would have asked the same thing had I been a mother in her shoes. That was a life experience I never wanted to have. "I told them the same thing because it's a small community. That the couple came to realize they weren't marrying for the right reasons."

"I see."

"The invoices for their fees will be in your email within forty-eight hours. I'll be cc'd so that the numbers match what I have. Of course, my fee is waived, Mrs. Abernathy."

"Nonsense, Taylor. I've already run the transaction. You'll see it in *your* account within twenty-four hours." She laughed.

"I don't know what to say."

"Say 'Thank you, Victoria.'"

The woman certainly had a way with her. "Thank you, Victoria."

"You're welcome."

"Have a good—"

"One more thing. I want to thank you for being at Crystal's side. I'm not sure she would have been able to tell me without your support. She didn't need to worry because I love my child, but I'm glad you were there. It meant a lot to both of us, Taylor."

The words stuck for a moment before I found my voice. "You're both welcome. I was happy to be there. Please give Crystal a hug for me."

"Good night, Taylor."

I stared at the dark screen. It had been a privilege to get to know them. To see matriarchal wisdom in one woman and finding out what authenticity felt like in the other. I flipped a couple of months forward on my calendar. *Send a note to Crystal.* The butterfly emerges from its cocoon in its own time. Crystal was just breaking free.

Breaking free. That's what I wanted to know from Kell. Was she serious about breaking free of every social mandate and conventional thought she ever knew, to feel free? I mean, really free. If so, it was probably for the first time in her life. Damn it. I wanted to be the person who helped her step through the door. And whether or not I had my own motive standing side by side with chivalry, I wanted her in my life, one way or another. This was one time I had to trust that we were together now. Kind of. I wasn't going to let her slip away without doing everything I could to let her know how I felt.

CHAPTER NINETEEN

*K*ell, *I should have contacted you sooner. We need to talk about last night. Let me know if tonight works for you."*

Well, at least that was a Taylor I recognized. I pressed the replay number again. The words that came through were controlled, self-assured. That Taylor I could handle. What would happen if the Taylor from last night was who she was more often than not? I leaned against the counter and closed my eyes. I could feel her lips against my ear while her fingers were wrapped around my throat. And when she zeroed in on my clit, I nearly lost it. I opened my eyes and concentrated on breathing. Shit.

After I cruised through the glossary, I'd kind of skimmed over the other two, then admitted the overall principles and way of thinking were a bit over my head. I had more questions than answers and I couldn't help contemplating there was a reason Taylor had picked those particular books. The one that was easier to understand, although how accurate it was remained in question, made me appreciate how much work a Dominant put into a dynamic. It was so much more than sex, but the power exchange was critical to both parties. Granted, I'd bounced around in each book, but Taylor couldn't possibly think I'd read them all since last night. If she did, she was a lot more demanding than I already thought she was. Maybe demanding wasn't the right word. Either way, I wasn't sure if that was how I wanted to start this journey. I needed some give and take. At least some compromise.

I picked up the books and flipped till I found the reference of who a submissive was. "…someone who dearly, desperately wants you to control them." Taylor definitely wanted the control, but did I want that for myself? I tapped in a quick message, my fingers flying over the virtual keys. Taylor wasn't the only one who had questions.

Yes, tonight works. My place seven o'clock. I'll order in. I hesitated. The message didn't speak warm and fuzzy at all. Maybe that was okay. I didn't want to bury myself beneath false pretenses. Taylor might have gotten my full attention, but we hadn't had a conversation about what I wanted or needed. I might have been naive when it came to the world of BDSM, but I wasn't about to step into the lion's den without any armor. That would be foolhardy no matter how badly I thought I wanted more of what Taylor had to offer.

❖

Papers were scattered over my desk. Files were left untouched. Today had been the day from hell with one catastrophe after another. One of the ovens in the kitchen went on strike, leaving us one short with a nearly full house of guests. Louie had adapted a lot of the dishes offered, but there was still a lot that couldn't be made. The repair person said it would be a month before the part would arrive, so I did the only viable thing and ordered a replacement that would arrive in two days. Not the best solution, but the best I could come up with.

Then one of the guests overflowed their soaker tub. Luckily, the water had only leaked into a minimally used storeroom, but it would still require an insurance claim and I wasn't thrilled about having to deal with one more inspection. At least that wouldn't happen today. After rubbing my eyes, I squinted at the clock. It was almost six. Where the hell had the day gone? I recalled a bottle of sauvignon blanc chilling in the refrigerator. A full glass and a hot bath would be a perfect way to end this hellacious day. All I had to do was decide what I wanted for dinner and pick it up on the way home. *Fuck.* Taylor was coming and I was supposed to order dinner. Fuck, fuck. I shoved my laptop and planner into my leather bag before slinging my purse over my shoulder. No time for dawdling now. There were only two restaurants on my way home. A Thai that was passable, and a pizza joint that was good but usually took forever. Since time was of the essence, I called an order in for a half dozen of my favorite dishes. They were quick to get food ready. I wanted a few minutes to organize my thoughts before Taylor, who was punctual to a fault, showed at my door.

I raced through the door fifteen minutes later, turned the oven to two hundred degrees, and slammed the containers in. Off to the races. I couldn't believe I stopped the whole process to consider what I should wear. It was a weeknight and I'd worked all day. My go-to was a pair of leggings and a T-shirt. Wanting to look a little more put together, I opted for a casual but nice pullover shirt, but all my sleep bras were in the laundry. Why they were called that I couldn't comprehend. Who in their right mind slept wearing a bra unless a woman had such large breasts they could hurt themselves by just rolling over? Taylor would have to deal with my tits being free.

A few minutes later, the table was set, and I was eyeing that bottle of white in the fridge when the door chime rang. I'm not sure why I became a bundle of nervous energy when I'd not five minutes earlier given myself a stern pep talk about being calm and asking why Taylor did what she did last night. All my strategy went out the window when I opened the door to find her standing there with a bottle of wine, looking hot enough to melt glass. She almost smiled.

"Good evening, Kell."

Damn her. Why did she have such a visceral effect on me? "Come in." I stepped back to make room. Her cologne drifted to me, and I inhaled deeply. The scent was bright, almost citrus-like. I'd expected something darker, more robust, considering how she carried herself, but like the nail polish that shone at the tips of her fingers, Taylor was anything but predictable. She turned and did nothing to hide her attention as her gaze traveled from where our eyes met over my chest, where she paused long enough that she knew there was only one layer between my erect nipples and her before continuing downward. I wish I had some smart remark to stop her from looking at me like she owned me. I didn't want to stop her.

"I hope you like Thai," I said as I headed to the kitchen, giving her a perfect opportunity to view my ass. I may have put a little bit extra in the sway of my hips.

"Thai is one of my favorite go-tos."

I hid my heated face in the cupboard as I selected a wine glass though they were all the same. "What's another?" I set it on the counter next to mine, and when I turned, Taylor was closer.

"Sex."

Registering what she said took me a long beat. Maybe I hadn't heard her correctly. "Pardon?"

"Sex is my other go-to."

"Oh. Really?" Was that the best I could come up with?

"Really." Taylor held up the wine, acting as though she hadn't just dropped a bombshell. "Should I open this?"

Thank goodness my brain kicked in. "Yes, please." I rummaged in the drawer for the corkscrew and gave myself a stern warning to keep my shit together. I wasn't mad about what happened, but Taylor had some explaining to do and I needed to stay on track, not get sidelined by my suddenly wide-awake libido that included a number of unconventional behaviors. When I turned around holding up the corkscrew like a baton, Taylor was already pouring. It was then that I noticed the screw top. She handed me my refilled glass, smiled, and held hers aloft.

"To answers."

It would have been senseless for me to act as though I didn't know what she meant. "To answers." We clinked glasses and the pure sound somehow resonated with me in a way I'd never thought of. Taylor's voice brought me back.

"Is there anything I can do?"

Do? Hadn't she done enough by flipping my brain upside down in showing me a world that might otherwise have remained nighttime fantasies for me?

"Kell?"

"Hmm?"

"Can I help with dinner?" Taylor's gaze revealed she knew exactly what I was thinking.

"Yes, you can." I pulled a tray from the narrow cabinet next to the stove, then removed the cookie sheet out of the warm oven. The food wouldn't be steaming, but warm enough to enjoy. I filled the tray with containers, not bothering to use serving bowls. "Hope you don't mind eating a bit Bohemian." I handed her the tray.

"Not at all. In fact, I never understood the need to dirty more dishes when containers do the job." She smiled warmly and took the tray to the table.

I pretended not to notice how good she looked in tight jeans and a rayon, plaid shirt, unbuttoned low enough to reveal a shadow of her breasts. I wasn't looking. I wouldn't have thought Taylor would wear flannel, and I was right for the time being. The shirt was a little dressy without looking out of place. Silverware was already on the table, so using that as an excuse to stall sitting across from her wouldn't work. I picked up our glasses, took a steadying breath, and went to face the inevitable. Taylor stood next to the chair I normally sat in. "I hope you're hungry." I held out her glass.

"I'm always hungry."

The look in her eyes told me she wasn't talking about food, and an onslaught of visions from the night at the Play Palace flashed in front of me. "Good." The word came out raspy and barely audible. Taylor shared a lopsided grin and disappeared, then returned with the bottle of wine and poured modest amounts into our glasses, though mine required more. I began removing lids and Taylor began to do the same. When her fingertips brushed the back of my hand, I pulled away as though I'd touched fire. In a way, I had. Taylor was dangerous in all the most delicious ways.

"What are you afraid of?" Taylor sat back, took a small drink, and continued to stare.

Once more at a loss for words, I decided I had nothing to lose. "Let's fix our plates first." When Taylor didn't move, I pressed on. "Please?"

Taylor was so still, it was eerie. She shook out her napkin. "There's a lot of food here. Are you inviting others to the party?" She waved her hand over a dish and inhaled. "The aromas are very savory." She began to scoop, holding out her hand. "Are you willing to allow me to fix your plate?"

Was Taylor asking a question outside of food? I couldn't be sure. I wasn't sure of much these days when it came to her expectations. Everything was so jumbled. "Yes. Thank you."

"I'm going to assume you ordered what you like, but if there's something you don't like you'll need to tell me." She placed a small amount of each offering onto my plate.

"Thank you."

"You're welcome." Taylor repeated with her plate, then began to sample, taking her time as she chewed. "This is really good."

It was impossible for me to wait any longer. "Why did you back me against the gate?"

"Because you pissed me off," Taylor said without preamble. "I don't answer to you, Kell, nor do you have any right to know where I was or with whom."

I blinked several times. Her words were firm and left no room for negotiation and I assumed this was how she treated her submissives, too. "So I gathered." I put my fork down, my appetite gone. "It that how you treat—"

"No, you're wrong. That isn't how I treat my submissives. I'm firm about behaving and listening, and I can be forceful at times, but I respect my submissives because they respect me. That's what made my temper flare. Your lack of respect to me." Taylor took a drink. "There's a fine line between what can be asked and what can't, but you and I aren't in a dynamic and you don't have the same privileges a submissive would have. Even then, they are earned."

I mulled over what I could remember about her, but there were still questions. "Do you ever kiss?"

Taylor's face fell, her gaze downcast. "Kissing is intimate."

"And you're not into intimacy?" She folded her napkin, sat back, then crossed her legs.

"Some submissives fall in love with their Dominant. Once that line is crossed it's hard to break, and when the dynamic ends, they can be emotionally scarred. That result can lead to their resisting having subsequent dynamics, which doesn't work because their true nature has been revealed."

Something about Taylor's explanation didn't sit well with me. "So you want a detached submissive?" She didn't know much about what she wanted but detachment wasn't it.

"Not detached so much as emotionally controlled. Falling for a Dom who might turn out to be different than what a submissive is looking for can lead to bad feelings and resentment within the dynamic, and that's never a good thing."

I didn't picture Taylor as a coward, but it sounded more like she was the one who was afraid of developing an attachment to her sub than the other way around. "I'd still like to be kissed by you." I got on my knees. If Taylor wanted submission I was going to give her my version of it. "Will you please kiss me, Sir?" I wasn't sure where the request would lead, especially since I clearly saw the struggle it created for Taylor, but I wanted to feel those lips against mine.

Taylor grabbed a fistful of my hair then bent my head back as she growled. Her teeth traced along the column of my throat, scoring my tender flesh. I wanted to watch her, but Taylor had a firm grip, my head faced away. She worked her way along my chin with nips just hard enough to keep me grounded to the present. When she was done, she brought my head up and slid her lips over my parted ones then slipped her tongue inside. Licking. Swiping. Searching. For what I didn't know and didn't care. Then she was gone. My chest heaved. My panties were soaked. My mind…well…it had temporarily gone MIA.

"Fuck. You can kiss."

Taylor shrugged in a non-committal response. She lifted me to my feet. "It was just a kiss."

Our conversation wasn't going at all like I thought it would. I needed intimacy and it sounded as though Taylor wasn't accustomed to that particular act in her previous dynamics. For better or worse, Taylor was the one who would dictate what happened between us. Maybe it was time I stopped fighting it and saw where things led.

❖

Shit. There wasn't one part of the kiss that felt out of place, and that's what was so disconcerting. I didn't kiss my submissives because I knew they'd misinterpret my intentions. I needed to keep some emotional distance to maintain control. Kell made letting my guard down easy without even trying. She was so sexy. So enticing. I didn't doubt she could calm the raging beast inside. But I not only wanted to be inside her body, I had to be inside her head, too. I needed to know her motives.

"What do you want, Kell?" I was on the verge of losing control again. The conversation needed to go in a way that would serve me rather than force me to make excuses for my behavior.

"I'm not sure what you mean?"

"Don't be coy. You know exactly what you want." I leaned forward, making sure Kell was looking at me. "Tell me."

Kell's cheeks pinked. "I want to be one of those women." Her eyes closed and she took a deep breath.

"You'll never get what you want if you try to make me guess." I waited patiently, back in control.

"I want to be on my knees for you and to see what it feels like to be submissive."

Finally, we were getting somewhere. "What does that mean for you? What does being on your knees represent?"

Kell threw her hands up, clearly frustrated. "If I knew I wouldn't be wondering what all of these damn emotions I'm feeling are, now would I?"

I stood and went to her. There were times when every Dominant needed to calm a frantic submissive. Just because Kell wasn't mine didn't mean I should sit by and watch her suffer. It had nothing to do with my parallel desire for Kell to be more than a submissive, I wanted her as a partner. An honest to goodness, full-time partner. A total power exchange in every sense of the word. That was new territory for me. *Baby steps.* Kell wasn't the only one whose thoughts were confusing. "Hey." I took her hands and helped her sit. "It's okay to not know everything you want at once. Focus on the things you do know. Okay?" Tears pooled in her eyes. I kissed her forehead, then held her at arm's length. "Would you like to try?"

"Yes?"

"Is that a question?"

"No, I want to try." She brushed away unshed tears and cleared her throat.

"Good. First things first. When you address me it is with respect by using my title. May I please try kneeling, Sir?" I expected Kell to balk. Instead, I could see her attempting to wrap her head around the words. She repeated the phrase.

"You may." I held her hands to support her. Then she lowered to both knees. "How does being there feel?" Her gaze traveled upward, momentarily stopping at my crotch. My clit grew.

"It's a different view."

"Do you like it from where you are?"

"Yes."

"Try again." She looked confused for a moment.

"Yes, Sir."

"That's better." I held her chin. "That would be your view a lot if you were my submissive."

"Now what?" She rushed on. "Now what, Sir?"

"You'd ask what you could do to please me, or if you could suck me."

"Can I suck you, Sir?" Kell asked, eyes questioning.

"May I please suck you, Sir?" Once she corrected her question, it was my decision if I would allow her to continue or deny her what she asked for. "Unbuckle my belt and expose my crotch."

Kell did as instructed then sat back on her haunches. She met my gaze. "I don't know what to do next."

Patience was a signature characteristic of a Dominant who knew what they were doing and understood a submissive's hesitation. The important thing to remember was that part of my role included encouraging and guiding a submissive to realize their potential and actively engage in wanting to be submissive to their Dominant.

"Do you know how to give oral sex?"

Kell nodded. "Yes, of course."

"Take my clit into your mouth and gently suck. Don't pull too much. Use your tongue." Her gaze turned hot, and she paused for the briefest moment before placing her hands on my hips and pressing her mouth to my clit. The feel of her wet, warm tongue against my feverish flesh after having fantasized about this very scene so many times had me on the edge of orgasm. I didn't want it to end here. Not like this and not when Kell might decide this wasn't anything she wanted. I let her continue a few more minutes. "Stop."

Kell looked up, confused. "Am I doing something wrong?"

"No. I don't want you to continue without an agreement, and you aren't collared."

"What do you mean?"

Backing away, I buckled my pants and took a minute to settle my thoughts of wanting to get off on her mouth. I wanted Kell's submission, but it had to be with her full understanding, not by talking her into something she didn't fully mentally grasp. As much as the attraction continued to grow, I wasn't prepared to answer all her questions tonight. Some she deserved to know.

"A dynamic is based on boundaries and clearly outlined intentions, guidelines, rules, and understandings. We don't have an agreement, and you aren't wearing my collar."

"A collar," Kell said. "Like the kind those women wore in the Play Palace?"

"Yes, like those or something similar. It's an outward sign of being owned or under consideration, and that you aren't free to be submissive with anyone else." I could see Kell struggling to comprehend. "It's a complicated world to understand only because the terms of a coupling, or dynamic, are out in the open and clearly stated, unlike other relationships." I held my hand out.

Kell stood. "You mean relationships in the straight world?"

"Not just the straight relationships. Almost every relationship except a D/s or other type of dynamic is that way. But the world of BDSM demands the tenets of safe, sane, consensual relations. If that doesn't exist, it's abuse, and no one in a relationship wants to admit they're in an abusive one."

"That's sad."

"It is, but that's reality." My concern for Kell's emotional state came to the forefront. "How are you feeling?"

Kell's cheeks flushed. "You mean aside from being turned on and left hanging?" She laughed. "You know what just happened was a tease."

It was true and I knew it. "What else are you feeling?"

"I want to know more. Do more." She extended her hand. "May I touch you?"

The ways that I wanted her to touch me were numerous. "Yes." She took my hand and I let out a breath, though admitting it was more out of disappointment than relief would have to come later.

"I can't deny you've gotten my attention in so many ways and I am grateful. Please don't leave me in limbo."

Briefly, I closed my eyes. Maybe my fantasies with Kell weren't so far-fetched after all. "There are many ways to interpret my world, and I'm only one person with my own view of it all."

"That may be true, but I'm only asking for yours."

"Let's finish our wine and I'll answer what I can." Knowing that Kell was not only curious but curious about me gave me a thrill I couldn't compare to any other and was a known basic need for a lot of Doms. We thrived on the focus of a submissive's attention meant only for each Dominant. Once she knew all my kinks and the submission I'd require, then the only thing that concerned me was Kell admitting her desire to learn more. Yet, I still wondered if she'd be willing to give up so much of her way of thinking to embrace the truest form of trust and unleash the full extent of her desires.

CHAPTER TWENTY

I noticed the woman who sits at the end of the bar seems pretty attentive. Anything I should know?" Maggie asked.

Was it that obvious? There was no sense trying to deny it since it was pretty clear. "She's not the only one interested."

"Oh. Do tell," Maggie said as she flipped burgers without even looking. She'd been doing this a long time.

"There's not much to tell. We've been on a few dates. There's definitely a mutual attraction." I shrugged as though it wasn't a big deal. "I think we're going to see where it goes." I'd been ravenously reading the books from Taylor, and the more I read, the more I wanted to explore and engage.

"Sounds to me like you're enjoying it." She took the buns off the grill, then piled lettuce, tomato, and onion on one top and lettuce, avocado, and pickle slices on the other before adding a burger on the bottom. One had cheese, one mushrooms. Everyone liked something different.

"I am." I shared a smile, then picked up the plates to bring to the bar. Taylor had been firm on making sure we had clear boundaries in place before more physical interactions happened. She said she swore by the core tenets the lifestyle insisted on and she had no intention of going against them. Friday after work I would drive to her place, and we would review the agreement she promised to send by the end of today.

In the meantime, I had customers to tend to and more reading to do when it was slow. The more information I had on board the more I'd be ready for what Taylor would present to me. The discussion would be a formal type, where terms, conditions, and boundaries would be discussed at length. She wanted me to think about things I'd like to try or try more of. Things I didn't want to try at all, and things that would bring up bad or painful memories. Those questions weren't even close to any of the subjects my previous relationships had ever delved into. Even other couples I knew often weren't aware of past hurts and traumatic experiences. I doubt they even thought about it. I was guilty of the same thing. Maybe Brenda had been brought up in an overbearing or abusive home where she had no voice. Or maybe her inability for getting things done was more of a rebellious statement and her way of expressing her desire to not be told what to do. It wasn't an easy pill to swallow. Maybe I'd bring it up with Taylor.

The night flew by. With a steady flow of customers, I didn't have to work at keeping Taylor off my mind. Much. Maggie made the usual noise as she shut down the kitchen, and I shook my head at how quickly I'd adapted to things so foreign in such a short time.

"Good night, Kell." She gave me a squeeze. "I hope you and your friend have fun, whatever you do," she said with a wink.

After she left, I locked the door behind her and pulled all the money from the drawer except for the fifty dollars that was start-up. I jotted down the number of each denomination, tore the original from the pad, stuffed it in the bag, then dropped it down the chute.

When I looked up, I was standing in front of Jack's usual spot. He'd been MIA for my last two shifts before I remembered some kind of vacation with the guys he used to work with. Taylor had also been a no-show and I wasn't sure what to make of her absence. Maybe she had a play date. At least, I think that's what a casual BDSM interaction was called. There were so many terms, my head was spinning.

As I gathered my things, I recalled the night I'd accused Taylor of going to the Play Palace. It had been a mistake and Taylor had made sure I knew it. Not that I blamed her. The jealous flare had appeared out of nowhere. I wasn't a jealous person, so why now and why with Taylor?

With only my day job tomorrow, I'd have a chance to read. Always the student, I'd bought a five-subject notebook. Each of the first three were for the books Taylor had loaned me. The next one was for our discussions because I was sure there'd be many, and the final was for my own thoughts, questions, and reflections. There was only one entry in that part. "How did it feel to be told to be on my knees?" I wasn't sure about the on my knees part, but the way Taylor commanded me and then when her clit was revealed, the entire experience had left me aching in a place deep inside. Perhaps that was the answer to the emptiness that often washed over me. I had refused to give it space or time to grow. Whatever this thing was, I wasn't going to turn my back on it.

❖

"Hi," Taylor said as she stepped back. "Please, come in."

If I thought I'd been nervous around Taylor before, I was wrong in my assessment. Nothing compared to the swarm battling inside my stomach. "Thank you." I stepped inside the open foyer that wasn't grand so much as inviting. The thick, dark overhead beams brought the ceiling down from the vast, open space. It was intimate and warm. "You have a lovely home."

Taylor waved for me to follow her, her bare feet silent on the slate before moving onto aged hardwood floors. I might have been expecting them to creek, but the flooring was quiet. "Thanks. It's nothing special, but it's mine." She pointed at a sectional couch that had to have had at least ten pieces, maybe more. "Make yourself comfortable. I'm going to bring drinks."

"Can I help?"

"Thank you, it's already done." Taylor disappeared through an archway, leaving me to imagine what the rest of the rooms looked like.

I set the charcuterie platter on the center of the dark, square coffee table. Since I'd had to work all day, I called in a favor from Louis. The result was spectacular, and I was glad he hadn't overdone it. Left on my own for a minute and needing a distraction, I smoothed my hand over the worn, polished wood. It matched the beams overhead that mirrored the ones from the entry. The contrasting color with the saddle brown couch was perfect, as were the dozens of throw pillows of different shapes, sizes, and colors that adorned the space.

"Here we are." She set down a tray containing a bottle of wine, two goblets, plates, and woven napkins. She poured into each glass, held one out for me, and raised hers. "To clarity, honesty, and boundaries."

The first sip sat on my tongue long enough for me to pull the subtle hints of pepper, oak, and currant from it. It would accompany the platter offerings exquisitely. "This is really good."

Taylor's smile appeared relaxed. Not that she didn't normally appear that way, but other times I'd seen her, I could sense an intense energy that simmered under the surface. Like molten lava buried beneath the serene landscape. "It's one of my favorites. I'll give you a bottle before you leave."

The casual way in which she made the offer might have appeared pretentious to anyone else, but I knew Taylor enough to know it was genuine. "Thanks." I pulled the wrap off the tray. "I wasn't sure what you'd like." I glanced at the assortment Louis had chosen, then at Taylor. She reached for my hand. Hers was warm and a delightful mix of soft and firm, much like Taylor herself.

"You'll never have to guess because I'll tell you."

A little while ago I'd been ravenous and worried I'd dive into the food like someone who hadn't eaten in days. Now all I wanted was for Taylor to keep touching me everywhere and in all the ways I'd begun to dream about. All the dark, forbidden ways that a respectable woman would never dream, or fantasize about. At least, that was what I had believed not so long ago, and what society expected. Since meeting Taylor, I'd stopped pretending I didn't want to feel more than the everyday kind of acceptable sex that others got so worked up about. Yet, when I slowed down enough to examine my wants and desires, I wondered if they were anything Taylor would be interested in. What could I bring to a dynamic that she couldn't get from someone else? What else would Taylor expect? Everything couldn't be sexual, right? Sure, I wanted sex and to try new things, but there would be more than sex in a dynamic, wouldn't there? And would Taylor, with all her experience, take the time to discover what those things were for me?

"What are you thinking about?"

After taking a deep breath, I forged ahead. "About the nasty, sexy things I want you to do to me."

Taylor squeezed gently. "Tell me about them."

Heat infused my cheeks, my sex clenching. "I'm not sure I can." Breaking the physical connection might have helped, though I didn't want to at all.

"It wasn't a question. It was a command."

The air left my lungs. Taylor's voice wasn't menacing, but it left no room for guessing who was in command. How had she perfected the tone that made me sit up and take notice? Granted, there was something about her demeanor and her forbearance that couldn't be ignored, but she couldn't be serious. However, one look into her eyes sent a shiver through me and I knew there'd be consequences if I didn't respond.

"I was thinking about you tying me down and taking me in so many different ways that I'm wet and throbbing." When Taylor slid her hand away I almost whimpered at the loss.

"Good." She lifted her wine to her lips. "Fix my plate, then yours." She sat back, apparently content to watch what I would do.

My hands trembled as I worked, putting a selection of meats, cheeses, olives, and crackers onto a plate before starting to set it in front of where she sat.

"Good girl."

A shiver of excitement coursed through me as I set it down. The power of Taylor's words was intoxicating, and I couldn't move.

"What did I say?"

Panic churned in my gut, souring the wine. What had she said? I'd been lost in the fantasy of being tied down and helpless. I'd gotten the main message from her, but exact words were just out of grasp at the moment. She leaned forward, her eyes focused and bored into mine. She grasped my chin firmly.

"Paying attention to everything I say is another thing you'll have to learn. Understand?" She was still as my mind raced to fill in the blanks.

"Yes."

"What?" Her fingers tightened.

Her grip was starting to get uncomfortable. Just when I thought about pulling away, a previous conversation surfaced, and I knew what was missing. "Yes, Sir."

Taylor released my chin. "That's better." She stroked my cheek gently, then sat up, staying close. "Now think. What did I say about the food?"

That conversation felt like it happened hours ago. I didn't have a clue. "I'm not sure." I quickly added, "Sir."

"I would expect you to remember if you were my submissive." Taylor poured more wine into her glass, but not mine. "I told you to fix my plate first, then yours. I will always tell you the order to do things and I don't expect to have to say it more than once."

I quickly filled the plate in front of me, then looked up. Taylor came close once more and kissed my forehead.

"Good behavior will be rewarded."

A peaceful calm washed over me. It was so far removed from any other experience I'd had that there wasn't any way for me to put it to words.

Taylor picked out a piece of cheese, slowly chewed as though savoring the flavor. "How are you feeling?"

"Cherished." The word tumbled from my lips without forethought. "Why did you kiss my forehead?" I wasn't a child, but she'd called me a good girl. I'd read about the term in one of the books but couldn't recall the meaning.

"Because you'd done well and deserved to know." Taylor was clearly in her element. I was anything but.

"How will I know I've done what you expect?"

"You're not paying attention. I told you, you won't ever have to guess. If I tell you to do something, I'll also tell you how to do it, but after a while you will need to remember what you've been told. If I want something different from the usual, that's when I'll tell you so."

So many rules and so much to remember. "I don't think I'll ever be able to keep it all in order." I was good at organizing my thoughts, but what Taylor was explaining wasn't the way I usually thought about a relationship. What she was saying wasn't a vague reference, as was so often the case in other conversations. This was precise.

"If you decide to be a submissive in a dynamic, there will be things you'll need to do every day to help you remember not only your place, but how to perform your service." Her tone was controlled, not showing emotion but not fully void of it either. "Did I tell you to read the contract before tonight?"

Trepidation coursed through me. I got the distinct feeling she already knew the answer. "Yes, Sir."

"Did you?"

I chewed my lower lip, flicked my gaze away. It had been a couple of horrible days of work with not a minute to myself. "Not in total, Sir."

"Stand up." Taylor stood behind me, her lips near my ear as she pulled down my pants. "Disobedience will be met with discipline every time."

I opened my mouth, but before I could get a single word out, Taylor's hand connected with my ass. Once, twice, three times. The sting was intense but was followed by a soft rub that soothed my flesh.

"The next time you're spanked you will respond to each strike by saying, 'Thank you, Sir.' Do you think you can manage that?" Taylor sat and picked out an olive, then popped it in her mouth. "Pull your pants up, slut."

Maybe it shouldn't have, but the slur sent a shiver of excitement through me while I fixed my clothes. For some unwise reason, I faced her and fought against the urge to grin, failing miserably. "Thank you. Sir."

"If you think I'm playing a game, we're done here." Taylor finished her wine and my grin faded. The intensity of our encounter left no room for misinterpretation.

"I'm sorry, Sir."

Taylor crossed her legs, folded her napkin in precise thirds, then laid it over her thigh. "You have a new assignment, but before you begin I want you to think if a D/s dynamic holds any interest for you. It's not a fantasy for a quick thrill, or a different way to engage in sex. It's a lifestyle that includes a very different way of thinking and processing information from mainstream relationships. It's giving me, or another Dominant, full control over what happens in your day-to-day life and in the dynamic itself. It should be a total power exchange and a matter of unquestionable trust. You can't do this halfway. Someone will suffer and it would likely be you."

The amount of control and patience Taylor exhibited still amazed me. The whole idea that someone worked tirelessly to do what was best for their submissive was a foreign concept, and one I was just beginning to appreciate. Likely because of my misconception of the role of what a submissive was and how underrated their contribution could be. It was possible Taylor didn't see me as being able to fulfill my obligation in a dynamic. The thought was sobering. "Are you saying you don't think I'll make a good submissive?"

"Not at all. My only concern is that you don't pursue the lifestyle with eyes wide shut. It's demanding of time and energy, but I've found it to be more rewarding than the vanilla world could ever provide."

I let her words play through my mind, knowing if I took the next step there'd be no turning back. I wasn't a quitter, and I'd already come to the conclusion that Taylor was the person to lead me into the unknown with a surety I would not easily find in anyone else. There was a reason our paths crossed.

"What's the assignment, Sir?"

A slow smile spread on Taylor's lips. "I want you to read the contract I sent. Several times. Make notes and write down questions. If, and only if, you decide to engage in a dynamic with me we will have a formal discussion, set boundaries and limits, and swear to undertake the tenets of an approved D/s relationship. Do you understand?"

"Yes." I said the word with more conviction than I felt, but my desire wasn't in question.

"Since you're new to the lifestyle, there will be a period of training."

I opened my mouth, but Taylor's raised hand stopped me.

"You have enough to think about. Don't worry about anything but the contract."

"Yes, Sir." I nodded, pleased that I'd remembered how I was supposed to respond. Mostly. I'd do the assignment and hope that the result would be pleasing to us both.

CHAPTER TWENTY-ONE

Even an hour after Kell left, I could still feel the flesh of her ass against my hand as I drove around the city in a feeble attempt to quiet the unrest coursing through me. I wanted her more than I'd wanted any other submissive, and I'd had quite a few since becoming a Dominant.

The first act of discipline had been tempered by remembering she was under no obligation to bow to my whims and rules, but she had anyway. The bratty response had been natural. If she'd never been under the guidance and training of a Dominant, she wouldn't know how close she came to a much harsher punishment than the few taps she'd received for not properly addressing me. First shock, then realization had dawned on her beautiful face.

I wasn't angry Kell hadn't read the contract. Two jobs and who knew what other commitments she had could certainly make for a hectic life as it was, but if she signed on the dotted line, she'd have to adjust her schedule to accommodate the time I required from a sub. A decade earlier there'd been a year or so when I juggled three submissives at the same time. It had been a fun experience and I learned a lot about myself as much as my style of dominance.

For a brief moment I thought about stopping at the Play Palace. My energy was still high, but at a level that I no longer felt frantic, which was good. The thought of anyone who wasn't Kell touching me, or me fucking someone other than her, held no appeal. How strange was that? Like, had that ever happened since I'd stated my identification as a Dominant? My phone rang, startling me from the fantasies that were morphing into the one I fashioned with Kell as a key player. Les's number flashed. This couldn't be good news.

"Simpson."

"Hey. Am I disturbing you?"

"You're disturbing all right, but no, I'm driving home. What's up?"

"Melonie Walsh committed suicide." Les spoke quietly, a reverent tone in her voice that was reserved for serious situations. Melonie was one of our caterers. Her business made some of the most flavorful food I'd ever sampled.

"What? How?" I pulled into the garage and hit the button for the door.

"Information is sketchy, but Sharon said Melonie had broken down a couple of weeks ago about rising debt and not knowing what she was going to do."

The pandemic had fucked with hundreds of independent business owners across the United States, not to mention the entire world was suffering from a two-year downward trend. Recovery was slow and resources were limited. Every business that managed to go on was short-staffed. The economy had not only lagged behind, but the greedy companies were only interested in turning a profit, even if it meant squeezing the little guys until they couldn't breathe.

This situation was personal now. Nothing made sense. "Why didn't she talk to one of us?" The Daddy Dom in me, the side that cared for and encouraged and protected, wanted to right the tragic wrong.

"Taylor," Les said softly. "Whatever was going on, that decision was Melonie's."

Reasoning didn't mean shit to me. "Maybe if I'd been around more." It wasn't often I was self-deprecating. Senseless deaths brought out a deep-seated desire for vengeance that was ill-defined. A feeble attempt to right a wrong. I didn't regret the time I'd spent with Kell and whether those hours happened during the daytime or at night, I never would. The desire to nurture came naturally to me and whether it was someone I knew intimately or not never factored in.

"You always want to save the world, don't you?" Les knew me well, sometimes too well.

I wondered if I could save myself if the need ever arose. I chose to ignore the comment. "What about her family? She has…had…a couple of kids, didn't she?"

"That's the sad part for sure. A nine-year-old boy and a twelve-year-old girl. Her husband is a mess. He's keeping it together around the kids as best he can. I'm not sure how he's going to manage without her, or who might be able to take over the catering, if anyone."

My mind went into overdrive. "Do me a favor and set up a meeting with me and her husband as soon as possible. I think his name is Dale." I threw my stuff on the floor by the door and went to my computer. I didn't know what they would need, but I had to find out.

"Okay. What are you planning to do?"

"Whatever I can to take some of the burden off his shoulders." It was bad enough losing a loved one, but trying to pick up the pieces and keep a family from being torn apart in the process wasn't something I ever wanted to experience.

Money might not be the answer to everything, but it sure as hell helped with the practical stuff that would have been in Melonie's wheelhouse. Now everything was on Dale's shoulder, and he didn't have to bear it alone. No one should.

❖

Sunlight slashed through the curtains and fell across my face as I rolled over, groaning. I'd stayed up well after two in the morning, searching and researching about grieving families, the affect suicide had on children, what type of support most people needed. What I lacked in personal experience I'd try to make up for through financial resources. In some circumstances, money did make all the difference in the world. Though it was Saturday, I wanted to get moving. Les had sent an early morning text reassuring me she'd get in touch with Dale today. I didn't have great hopes for seeing him this weekend, but by next week I'd have time to have a real plan in place.

After shuffling out to the kitchen, I flipped on the coffee and opened the patio doors. I reached high and raised on my toes, stretching to my full length. I missed morning yoga and sitting on the patio while sipping Café du Monde, being mindful of my surroundings and staying in the moment. As the business grew, my free time had shrunk. That needed to change. I owed it to myself not only to engage with my kink and the sex I had once solely existed for, but to do things that would bring me back to center. The metronome of my life had become erratic and the moments that thrilled me were barely a blink. The only thing that still held my interest was when I engaged in a scene with a familiar. I didn't even bother to shake up the play with a new partner every now and again. What was wrong with me?

Without taking time to consider what I was doing, I pressed the speed dial number with her name next to it. Three rings later, her voice came through and a place deep inside settled into a comfortable spot.

"Hi." Breathless, Kell hurried on. "Is everything all right, Taylor?"

I'd never called her randomly before today. "Not really. Are you free to come over?" We still hadn't ironed out the details of the agreement. The working copy was in Kell's hands. I didn't mind fast-forwarding a bit, and I hope she didn't either.

"Yes. I can be there in fifteen." Everything went quiet on her end, and I checked to make sure I hadn't lost the connection. "Can I bring anything?"

"You." I hung up. I wasn't in a good place and had almost added, "Please." Not that asking for what I needed was a bad thing, but I didn't want Kell to have an opinion that I'd become needy and weak. That wasn't what she needed, and the dynamic wouldn't last if that's what she was hoping for.

I ran the shower and jumped in for a quick scrub. Ten minutes later, the doorbell rang. Wearing my favorite jeans and a robe tied loosely around my waist, I went to answer it. Nothing could stop me from smiling. When the door opened, I knew I'd made the right decision.

"Hey," Kell said, her hand moving toward my cheek, but she stopped a few inches away. "What's going on?"

I pulled her inside, kicked the door shut, and pushed her against it. My hand at her throat pinned her in place. "I need certain things from you. You can say no, and I'll go no further, but if you say yes, I'm going to take you in whatever way I want." I used my free hand to squeeze and tug hard at one of her nipples, making her gasp, then groan. I ran my teeth along the throbbing pulse on the side of her throat. God, how I wanted to fuck her, taste her. *Know her.* My restraint was thready at best. "Before you say yes, I want to hear your safe words. It's okay to use them if something's not working for you as long as you remember one will slow me down, the other will stop what I'm doing immediately." I loosened my grip on her throat.

"I read the document. I know what you're saying, Sir." Kell's voice was raspy and deep, as though she were the one fighting for control. "The answer is yes, Sir."

Fuck. "What are your words?"

"Yellow to slow down. Red to stop."

They weren't imaginative but they'd worked in the past. "Take your clothes off." I put a few steps between us. I wanted to watch her reveal herself without the temptation to touch.

"Here?" Kell glanced around nervously.

"Now." My focus felt like lasers pointed at her, and I knew that Kell knew I wasn't to be questioned. She began slowly, whether on purpose or because she thought it was going to turn me on wasn't clear. I'd talk to her later about that. Once they were piled around her on the floor, she stood still and glanced down the hallway. That's not where I wanted to fuck. I turned her swiftly and pressed her against the wall. "Spread your legs, hands out." I slid my fingers through the folds of her cunt. "Such a wet slut." My lips were next to her ear. "You want me to fuck you, don't you?" She whimpered. "That's not an answer." Two hard spanks got her attention.

"Yes."

Three more spanks followed. I took my time with them to let the sting settle in between each strike. "Try again."

"I don't—"

Two more spanks. "Did I say to talk back?" I grabbed her chin. "Are you sure you read the agreement?" Kell nodded. "Think about how you're responding to me." I saw the second it clicked.

"Yes, Sir."

"Better." She was likely reeling with a mix of pain and excitement, but it was not a reason to let Kell be contrite and disobedient. "Turn around. On your knees." Just because she wanted to get fucked didn't mean she was going to be. "You know what to do." This time it didn't take her long to figure out what I meant and she started to unsnap my jeans, the ones I'd picked to slow things down. Once she had them open, I snaked my fingers in her hair. "I want you to be a good girl and eat me like it's your last meal. Understand?"

Kell blinked several times and nodded. "Yes, Sir."

"Good girl." I let go and stood still. As much as I wanted her to place her trust in me, I had to trust in her eagerness to please. That was an aspect of the power exchange that would propel us forward. She parted my hair and licked my clit. Oh yeah, that's what I needed. Her tongue worked my flesh and her lips pulled and sucked at me. Even though I drifted into the sensations, I stayed mindful. Kell needed my reassurance as much as I needed her service. A Dominant was not only expected to guide through control, but also by praise. "You're eating me so well." Her eyes softened as she looked up, and she moaned against me. If she kept that up, I was going to come. I wanted to be naked and lying down when that happened. "Stop." She let go with a loud pop.

"Did I do something wrong?" A beat passed. "Sir."

I'd forgive the transgression. This time. "No." I took her hand and pulled her along behind me. We stood next to the bed, and I could tell Kell wasn't sure what to do next. I wouldn't leave her hanging for long. "Undress me." A moment of surprise crossed her face before she settled in and her fingers began to undo the sash of my robe, her eyes downcast. "Head up." When she complied, I continued. "You aren't being punished and you did nothing wrong. Eye contact lets me know you're mindful of what you're doing. That pleases me."

"Thank you, Sir." Kell continued to work at my clothes.

She was learning quickly, and I knew how my desire to own her had grown. I'd recognized her potential from the very beginning, though Kell hadn't had an idea what she was looking for at the time. I questioned how ethical the things I'd done had been. It wasn't as though I'd coerced her to go to either establishment. There'd been nothing wrong with not telling her my true nature until she had some idea on her own. The real reason was a sudden fear of rejection. That wasn't an emotion that I'd felt in more than a decade, so what kind of spell had Kell woven around me to make me get caught up in wanting to use her for my sexual pleasure and to punish her for either the lesson or to entertain my sadistic side. I lay on my back. The cool sheets beneath me helped me refocus on what I was going to have Kell do next. "Show me you know what I want."

Kell slow crawled over the side of the bed and settled between my thighs. "Like this, Sir?" She sucked my clit between her soft, hot lips.

Fuck. I grabbed her chin. "Don't play games. Don't ask questions you know the answer to. If you do it again, you'll be punished."

Kell swallowed hard, all the brat out of her. "Yes, Sir."

I moved her head to my crotch and settled back, confident that she knew who was in charge. Her hot mouth covered me, her tongue swiping over my hard clit. She didn't need direction. Intuitively, she stroked with the perfect pressure and in the way I enjoyed. It wasn't long before the tingling began to spread in my abdomen. I held her in place and gently thrust as I thought about all the ways I wanted to use her holes for my pleasure, but also for her pleasure, too. Kell held my thighs and moaned as I came, the perfect combination for my particular brand of kink. I enjoyed coming in a woman's hot mouth.

"Good girl," I said, giving her the praise she deserved for servicing my need. Well, her proposed service. We had yet to sign on the dotted line and I used wanting to get off as an excuse to show her what I expected. Before we went any further, and I definitely wanted to go further, a contract must be an agreement of terms…the consent part. I'd make sure it was safe and sane. It was time for the conversation we should have had a couple of nights ago. "Let's get something to drink. Then we can talk about the contract." If Kell was disappointed by not being touched, she didn't show it. We had work to do, and I wouldn't avoid my duty as a Dom any longer. I hoped Kell was as interested as I was in pursuing our dynamic.

Chapter Twenty-two

My heart pounded in my chest. Taylor had a firm handle on how she dominated, and although I was still clueless in many aspects of the BDSM world, I liked how her dominance made me feel. The part I wasn't thrilled about was being left sexually frustrated, but maybe denial was also part of a Dominant being in control. One thing I was certain of, Taylor would clear up any reasons for the hesitation I had. In the meantime, I tried to come up with my own questions because, honestly, there were so many I could barely keep them all in my head. Taylor put her clothes on. Mine were by the front door, leaving me feeling vulnerable and exposed.

"You may get dressed now. I'll meet you at the dining room table."

Once she was gone, I scooted off the bed and retrieved my clothes after a quick detour to the bathroom. I groaned at how slick my slit was. I found Taylor with her laptop, a couple of pads of paper, and pens. Bottles of water and a plate of fruit rounded out the display. She gestured to the chair adjacent to where she sat.

"Have a drink and something to eat. Write down any questions you can think of, then we'll get started." She tapped away at the computer, jotted on her pad, and drank her water.

The three or four questions I managed were inconsequential, but it was a starting point of how to get more comfortable with the opening conversation. Taylor appeared content to let me have whatever time I needed. I thought about how much I'd enjoyed eating her and if that was an act I'd be expected to perform often, so I added it to the list. After five minutes of trying to come up with additional questions, I put down the pen.

"Are you ready to start?"

"Yes, Sir." I was anxious to find out how I'd done.

"I'm going to read each section. Be mindful of the language and the meaning behind each. If you have questions, ask. You won't know what's expected or if you understand what's required if you don't ask. Your understanding is important."

She began reading. Her voice was smooth and her tone calm, but the inflection made the words stick. I stopped her several times. "When you say the submissive shall have no other dynamic outside of this D/s without first discussing with the Dominant, what does that mean? Is there always more than one?"

"Some in the lifestyle have more than one dynamic. Whether they are all D/s or something else is a personal preference." Taylor was quiet for a minute. "You might decide you want play partners. They're people you might want to try impact play with or engage in a role playing type scene with. All of which we would discuss beforehand."

"Will we be going to the club to play?" I wouldn't mind seeing more examples of kinks.

Taylor looked off. "Occasionally, but not on a schedule or regular basis. I took you there so you could see it's not as intimidating as people outside the lifestyle would have you believe." She finished her wine. "Besides, if you wanted to be tied up, I can take you to my version of a dungeon."

I laughed. Taylor wasn't laughing.

Once more I was struck by the details of the agreement. "So if you wanted to have a play partner, we would talk about it first?"

"No. I would likely tell you that I was going to play, but we wouldn't discuss it. Also, if I were to take another submissive or have additional dynamics, I would tell you." Taylor waited while I tried to digest the explanation. "A Dominant doesn't answer to her submissives. They answer to her, or him."

"So, I'm going to be one of many?" That didn't sit well. We hadn't made our dynamic official and already this was a point of contention.

"Kell, I don't want you to worry about what may or may not happen at some point. I'm looking forward to our dynamic, should you decide to sign. There's no one else under my consideration. Okay?"

For now. That's what Taylor was saying. Did it make sense for me to get tangled up in a detail that might never happen? It was okay to not be happy with that, but what if I were the one who decided to spread my wings? Would I want Taylor to clip them? My annoyance had more to do with learning how to be comfortable with a wide-open, no hidden agenda relationship than it did with the actual idea of Taylor needing or wanting others. I nodded. Taylor must have seen my hesitation.

"Just because I can have more, doesn't mean I'm looking to. Trust my commitment to you. It's all there." Taylor pointed to the pages between us.

I knew that it weighed more than any other arrangement I'd have. Even though the language was straightforward, the meaning behind them wasn't always clear to me. So I asked. Taylor was patient and it was so good to be able to be open with her while knowing there wasn't a hidden agenda to deal with. We took a break before reviewing the appendix section.

"I want to apologize to you for not telling you up front where we were going those first few nights. That was a shitty thing to do to you. You deserve to know what you're getting into and to give you a chance to decline." Taylor tapped her pad with her pen. "I made assumptions about you and that was also wrong of me." Her brow was furrowed. This was the first time I'd witnessed what could only have been worry on her face. I got the feeling that apologizing for embracing her dominance wasn't a common occurrence.

"Taylor, I could have asked. I trusted you and that I'd be safe, and I was." I thought back to the leather club. "There were a couple of times I was caught off guard by some of the presentations of people and what they were engaged in, but that doesn't mean I wasn't interested."

"I appreciate that, but it doesn't excuse my poor manners. It's critical that you trust me in every aspect of our dynamic. From this day forward, if you decide to move ahead with the agreement, I will always be open and honest with you. There is no room for doubt in a BDSM relationship, unlike most vanilla relationships. That's what sets it apart from all that you're familiar with."

"I'm sorry, Sir. I'll try to remember." I didn't doubt that Taylor was serious about the moral codes that were important to her and to what we might share. I'd never had that kind of equal responsibility with any previous short- or long-term partners. In the space of a few weeks, Taylor had established a connection so deep, I couldn't even begin to consider not being with her in some type of a relationship. Friendship for certain, but I wanted more, and so did Taylor. A lightning strike of electricity coursed through me. That too, was new, and every minute was exciting.

"I accept your apology and hope we can move on from here."

"Thank you." I drank more and popped a grape into my mouth.

"Next is limits and triggers. Mine are in the contract and you fill in your answers under the submissive column."

I'd read over the entire contract twice. Taylor's limits were straightforward. No dildo or penile penetration either vaginal or rectal. She had no other limits listed. There were seven triggers, some of which I surmised were trauma-related. "Why don't you have any other limits listed?"

"Ask me a different way."

This was where I tripped up. "Do you have limits?"

Taylor shook her head. "Ask again."

Now I was totally confused. What did Taylor want that I wasn't giving? It took another few minutes before it sunk in. "Do you have limits, Sir?"

"That's better." She patted my cheek and smiled. "If I do have limits you don't need to know what they are because you won't be initiating anything on your own. I'll be telling you what to do and when."

These were the kind of answers I didn't know if I needed to respond to. I had no previous experience to gauge them against. I'd perused the pages in the appendix and knew the things I had no interest in trying, but there were a number of them that I thought I might enjoy, and we reviewed each one I had questions about. When we were done, I sat back. I was wet and wanting to be touched in all the ways that were checked off.

"How are you feeling?"

My face heated. How could I express my darkest desires to Taylor? What would she think of me in light of, or despite, knowing about what they were? The thought must have been plainly written on my face because Taylor surmised as much.

"Kell, I don't want you to hesitate with me. This dynamic is going to be more open and honest than anything you've ever come across before. Granted, it's a new way of thinking, but it's not like you haven't had fantasies about carrying them out." Taylor paused and moved closer. "How are you feeling?"

I took a breath, then another. "Like I'm about to delve into something forbidden."

Taylor smiled as though she knew what I meant. "Perhaps, but nothing's forbidden in my world except non-consent." She glanced at the papers once again. "Are you ready to sign our agreement?"

The contract was only valid for thirty days. "What happens at the end of thirty days, Sir?" It hardly seemed long enough to know if the lifestyle Taylor was proposing would be something I'd do long-term or if I was just looking to satisfy a curiosity, though it didn't feel like the latter at all.

"We'll have weekly discussions as stated. If after the initial contract you want to extend its validity, we'll discuss that also." She produced another sheet of paper and slid it in front of me. "These are your daily chores. They are things to help you be your best self. They aren't part of the contract itself, but you can consider it a rider of sorts. You'll carry them out as instructed, and if you don't you'll tell me. It's both a way of reinforcing your submission, and reinforcement in showing that you are capable of more. It may not seem that way at first, but I assure you it will. Read them over and let me know if you have any questions." Taylor stood. "I'll be right back."

Her departure gave me a break from being scrutinized. Maybe that wasn't really what was going on, but my insecurities kicked in again as I thought of the possible ramifications of signing. I glanced over the list that appeared to be focused on caring for myself and had little to do with serving Taylor. They were outward signs of how I often sacrificed my own needs when something had to give. There were additional items such as eating right, doing some form of exercise or yoga, and taking time every day to be mindful. She'd been clairvoyant enough to include website links for examples and it made me chuckle.

Toward the bottom of the page was a list of "As time allows" items. Massage, manicure, hair stylist, etc. Again, the things I rarely carved out time for, but should have been doing before Taylor. She was a lot more than my naive idea of a Dominant. Those thoughts backed up against the possible pleasure I'd derive from Taylor, and I hoped I wasn't wrong for believing I was going to reap some sexual benefits from this arrangement, too.

Thinking that either of us might not want more than a few weeks together soured my stomach. Taylor brought in a carafe and fixings, along with two steaming mugs on an ornate serving tray. Then she set an onyx-and-pearl-barrel pen on top of the contract. The weight of the action wasn't lost on me, and I understood she viewed the entire process as reverential. This was, after all, her way of life, and it had strict boundaries and clearly defined lines of behavior and expectations.

"It's not too late to change your mind if you're having second thoughts."

I picked up the pen and turned to the signature page where her script was already on the line over the title Dominant and dated for today. Another line over the title submissive was calling to me and I added mine. It was thrilling and a bit scary, but I went with both feelings. I looked up and met Taylor's intense gaze.

"Thank you, Kell." She placed the document reverentially in a red folder marked Taylor *(Dominant)*/Kell *(submissive)*. "Starting immediately, the contract is binding. You'll do as I instruct without hesitation."

The room was suddenly too hot. I had to get out of there. I stood quickly, making the room tilt. Taylor was at my side immediately.

"Hey," she said as she guided me down onto the sofa. "Take a deep breath."

After I managed to stop the room from spinning, I tentatively smiled. "I'm okay now. Thank you, Sir." Was that right? Should I address her as such when in casual conversation? God, I was so confused.

"What happened?"

I laughed a bit. "You mean aside from my racing heart and pounding pulse, and the thought that I could fuck this up before it even began?"

Taylor chuckled. "You aren't going to fuck up anything because I won't let you."

It was in that moment that I felt an inner peace slide into place. Taylor would handle the big stuff, all I had to do was enjoy myself, provide what she wanted in the way of service, and focus my energies on things that made me feel complete. What a novel concept.

Chapter Twenty-three

The employee hours spreadsheet would be my nemesis. It took a minor miracle every two weeks to pull it together, but today all my powers of reason were nowhere to be found, as attested by the empty blocks dotting the form. A rapid knock on the door made me look up. "Come in."

"Hey, Kell, there's a woman at the front desk who says she needs to see you," Samantha leaned in the doorway.

I didn't have time for interruptions even though all I'd been doing for the past two days was daydreaming about all the ways Taylor would use my body for her pleasure. "Who is it?" Papers with every staff person's availability were spread across my desk and the scene annoyed my already on edge mood.

"She wouldn't say, but she said to tell you the dark horse is awake." Samantha cocked her head. "Do you know what that means?"

Heat traveled throughout my body, searing my skin. "Please tell her I'll be right there." I refused to look at Samantha after that. I didn't want her to ask anything else and I was pretty sure she would if she had any idea at all what I was feeling and thinking. I heard the door close and waited, counting to ten. Then I peeked into the hallway and hustled to the restroom. Taylor had settled on some code words. The dark horse phrase meant I was to remove my panties and finger my clit and not wash my hand. Funny how eager I was to do exactly as she instructed. We'd yet to engage in a scene since signing the contract, but it was her prerogative to call me, or call on me, whenever she wanted. I was to comply or deal with the fallout. I stuffed my panties as discreetly as possible in my bra and carried out her orders, amazed at how slick I'd become in the last two minutes.

Not wanting to keep Taylor waiting any longer than I already had, I hustled down the stairs and strode across the lobby with as much decorum as my shaky legs would carry me. I would have been able to pick Taylor out of a crowd without any difficulty because of the energy she emitted. Samantha gave a little chin raise in her direction as I neared the front desk, making the situation the tiniest degree less awkward. Taylor happened to turn my way at the same time.

"Hi, I'm Kell Murphy, operations manager." I stuck out the required hand, but fear set in, and I almost pulled it back. Taylor introduced herself then mouthed the word "trust." Her back was to the desk and the only person who could read her lips was lucky me. She took my hand, brought it to her mouth, and kissed my fingertips. Moisture ran from my clenched pussy, and for once I was glad the lobby was carpeted while I vainly attempted to clench my thighs. Certain Taylor was done, I tried to extract my hand, but her tongue darted out to taste what was there. I think I moaned, and panic grabbed my throat harder than Taylor had.

"Ms. Murphy, you may be familiar with my company, At Your Service. After all the mutual customers we've served, I thought it time we meet in person."

Smooth. That's the only word to describe how Taylor appeared. Like she didn't have a care in the world aside from the feigned conversation we were having. Maybe she didn't feel the visceral appeal for me that I had for her. I'd tasted her twice and couldn't wait until the next time. According to our contract, there would definitely be a next time, even if I didn't know when. I was almost as shocked by learning about the company she owned as I was at her appearance where I worked. Had we talked about specifics? I wasn't sure.

"Ms. Simpson, the pleasure is mine."

"Perhaps we could go somewhere to discuss...business matters?"

And just that quickly, it no longer mattered if I was on my home turf or not. Taylor would get what she wanted, or I'd pay the consequences. Whether that was true or not, I *wanted* to give her what she asked for. She'd promised discretion. When was the last time anyone had made me a promise I could count on? The answer was sobering. Never. No one except my parents had ever kept their promises. Granted, they didn't promise often, but they'd never gone back on the few they offered.

"Of course. Right this way." I waved my hand down the hallway, in the direction from which I'd come, and escorted Taylor that way. There was only one place I had a fair amount of privacy. My office had actual walls instead of glass windows and a lock on the door. I had an inkling I was going to be glad for both. It might have been my imagination, but it was as though Taylor could see beneath my skirt to my naked ass. When I opened the door, I breathed a sigh of relief. Taylor hadn't drawn attention to herself in the least. I, on the other hand, had been so turned on by her mere presence I was surprised I didn't drop to my knees right there in the lobby. "I thought my office would be best," I said. Taylor was on me like a predator, pushing me against the nearest wall and plunging her hand under my skirt.

"Good girl," she said, before squeezing my leaking pussy. "Needy slut. Is this for me?"

"Yes, Sir." The first time she'd called me her slut, I flinched. That reaction faded quickly when I remembered she'd classified me as a princess by day and slut by night. The meaning was everything I was coming to think of myself as. Well-behaved and professional during the day, and naughty as hell at night when I could shed one skin for another. Interestingly, Taylor encouraged me to embrace my authentic self all the time. I wasn't so sure the world, or I, was ready for the real me. She let go of my throat to pinch my nipple and I groaned.

"Do you like that, huh?" Taylor squeezed again. "Such a dirty girl."

My knees threatened to buckle. Taylor held me in place with a deep plunge into my pussy. Her pussy. Then my breath froze when there was a knock on the door. Taylor placed her hand over my mouth, removed her fingers and practically carried me to my chair.

"Lick my fingers clean."

At the same time, she handed me the phone, smoothed her clothes, then winked as she moved toward the door. The second it opened, and Samantha glanced at me, I babbled into the phone.

"I didn't mean to disturb your meeting. Would either of you like something to drink?" Samantha smiled sweetly, but I wondered if she had an idea what had been going on behind closed doors and wanted verification.

"I'd like a juice. Any kind will do. And Ms. Murphy will take…" Taylor paused as I made the sign for water, hoping she'd interpret the gesture. "Water," she said confidently. "One juice and a water."

Samantha smiled. "Right away, Ms…"

"Simpson. Taylor Simpson." She stuck out the hand I'd just been licking, and Samantha took it. Maybe the idea should have grossed me out, but it didn't. I almost burst out laughing.

Taylor closed the door behind her then turned. "Lesson two of trust." She strode to my side. "I will always handle every situation." She took the phone from me and set it in the cradle.

"Is that why you came here? To show me how to trust you?"

Taylor cocked a hip onto the corner of my desk, legs extended and crossed at the ankles. "That as well as being in the mood to watch you come. As soon as Miss Nosy is gone I'm going to lock the door and this time I won't stop." She walked toward the door and quickly pulled it open. Samantha nearly tumbled inside, uttering a low oath. I gave her props for not dropping the two bottles she held, cranberry juice in one, water in the other. "That was fast," Taylor said as she took both. "Efficient little thing, aren't you?"

I almost lost my shit at the look on Samantha's face. Somehow I managed to remember that an HR complaint was never a good thing. "Thank you, Samantha. Please let the receptionist know that I'm in an important meeting and not to be disturbed." I added, "Understood?" for emphasis. She had no idea if I was serious or kidding, and there was only one way to find out.

"Yes, Ms. Murphy." She glanced between us again before leaving.

"Fuck," I mumbled under my breath as I ran my hand through my hair.

"Exactly," Taylor said in agreement as she pulled me up and pushed my hips against the desk. She tapped my feet apart with the toe of her shoe and hiked up my skirt. "I've been waiting to do this since last night when I jerked off thinking about how you were going to taste." She slid her tongue along my soaked length. My head fell back, and I didn't try to hold back the moan. "Mmm, just as I imagined, only better." Taylor stroked my clit then darted away. The torturous pleasure made me squirm.

"Please, please." I tried to thrust my hips for more contact, but she held them down, adding a sharp, stinging slap to my cunt that made me wetter.

"How do you ask for what you want?"

"I need to cum please, Sir?" That wasn't right, but I was having a hard time thinking.

"No." Taylor stood, turned me around, and bent me over the desk. "Do you want me to fuck you?"

"Yes, please, Sir." Anything to relieve the pressure inside my abdomen that was like a volcano on the verge of erupting.

"That's what I thought, too." Taylor ran her fingers through my slickness. I sunk into the feeling until something larger filled my hole. "My cock feels so good inside your dripping pussy." She pulled out, tapped her dildo against me, then slid back in.

After three or four more times, I groaned. "Please, please?" I begged as I fought the urge to come.

"Don't you dare." Taylor pulled out, slapping my ass hard for emphasis. "Never come without permission."

I might have fallen if Taylor hadn't slammed back in and grabbed my hips. The mind-numbing pummeling was so damn good, I almost forgot the only way to get what I so desperately needed. "Please may I come, Sir?" I wasn't going to be able to hold on much longer. Taylor's mouth was at my ear, her hot breath on my neck as she grabbed a handful of hair and pulled back.

"Yes, you may, slut." She continued to pound into me. "Play with your clit and come on my cock." It was all the encouragement I needed before I started shouting. Taylor's hand covered my mouth as she rolled her hips. "Shhh…good girl. You don't want everyone out there to be jealous you got to have a midday fuck, do you?" She slow fucked me until my legs shook uncontrollably. She helped me to my knees and kissed my cheek. "You did well. Now clean me."

I looked around the office for something to use. I was just about to rummage in the credenza when Taylor stopped me with a hand on my shoulder.

"Use your mouth. Lick my dick clean of your cum."

I'd read so much about the power exchange and what it meant, that I felt a surge of pride. My Dom wanted my mouth on their dick. It was a request only made through trust and Taylor knowing I'd enjoy showing her how much I wanted to please her. Once she was clean, she pulled away and tucked her cock into her underwear, then patted my cheek. "You're learning quickly." She handed me the bottle of water, helped me up, and sat me in my chair. "Where are they?"

I pulled my panties from my bra and she smiled.

"You won't be needing these. I'm taking them as memorabilia." She started to leave but stopped. "Am I the first to fuck you in your office, Kell?"

"Yes, Sir."

Her smile grew. "Even better." She brought my panties to her nose and inhaled. "I better be the only one as long as I'm your Dom."

I nodded in response.

"I can't hear you."

"Yes, Sir."

"Mmm...hmm." Taylor left, closing the door quietly.

As I sipped water and pretended she hadn't left me a used and satisfied puddle, I couldn't help thinking what being with Taylor every day would be like, but then, she wasn't interested in me outside of our dynamic, and the hollow pit in my stomach felt like a chasm.

Chapter Twenty-four

I didn't plan the scene at the resort; it happened organically, like a lot of the scenes I played a part in. The strange thing was it felt like it wasn't a scene at all, but a page out of a book that was written about Kell and me. How our life might look in real life if we lived it twenty-four/seven. That was *my* dream scene. To be with the person who not only fulfilled my kink and fetish sides, but all the rest. Coming home, fucking, having a meal together, watching TV while she sucked me off or I fingered her. Sleeping with her tucked under my shoulder, head on my chest. An LTR wasn't even in the picture six months ago. Hell, I'm not sure it was on my radar three months ago, but it was there now, and I wanted it as much as I wanted to nurture the power exchange that was just developing between us.

As I pulled to the curb, I didn't see Kell's car and dread tightened my chest. I'd gotten a text from her early that morning saying she wished me a good day, but that was the last communication. It wasn't all that unusual not to hear from her a lot when she was working. I strode in and took my usual seat. Jack was in his spot three-quarters of the way down. He nodded and I returned the gesture. I looked for signs that Kell was there. Her signature seltzer with a twist of orange. Or her neatly stacked rags, bleached and ready for the night ahead. Nothing.

I almost gave in and asked Jack if he knew if Kell was working tonight when Pete, the owner, appeared from the kitchen and set a burger and fries in front of a customer at the other end of the bar.

"Hey, Taylor. Long time, no see." He wiped his hands on a towel and came closer. "What'll it be?"

I didn't want anyone to know I was anxious about Kell. "Surprise me, Pete, and have Maggie work some of her magic in the kitchen, too."

"You got it." Pete stuck his head in the back, and I heard Maggie's melodic voice chime in with a hearty laugh. "Not sure what you'll end up with, but I'm sure it will be good." He grabbed a couple of bottles—tequila, ginger beer, simple syrup—and put the top on the shaker. After that he smashed a maraschino cherry, stuck it on a long toothpick with a cube of candied ginger and a single mint leaf, and dropped it into the larger than average tumbler where he strained the concoction. He set it in front of me and winked. "My version of a Moscow mule. I call it the smarter ass." He chuckled and I joined him.

At first, I thought the combination would be too sweet, but as I took a second sip the sharp tang of ginger cut through the sweetness and the flavors mixed on my tongue in a surprisingly delightful way. "That's good," I said. I set the drink down and pushed on. "So what brings you here tonight? Someone call in sick?" I happened to catch Jack raise an eyebrow. There wasn't much he missed that's for sure.

"Kell has a situation at her day job. She said she'd be here by seven." He shrugged as he wiped glasses. "I had to meet the Realtor anyway, so it wasn't a big deal."

"Realtor?" I didn't like the sound of that, and my belly tightened.

"Yeah. I love this place. It's been in my family for more than sixty years. My wife…" Pete shook his head and took a breath. "She's not doing too well. I want to spend more time with her and take her on a long overdue adventure." Pete looked up, his eyes glistening with emotion. "I'm going to sell the Hole and take the money to make whatever time she has the best she could ever imagine."

I reached over the bar and grasped his forearm. I might not know all the details, but some things took priority, and his wife should definitely be one. "What about your employees?"

"I hope the new owner keeps everyone and hires a few more staff if they can find people willing to bartend or whatever, so everyone isn't stretched thin, like they are now."

"How much are you asking?" We talked about the details while I ate the roasted brussels sprouts with maple bacon dressing and enjoyed the cocktail. The price Pete was asking was fair market value from what little I knew. I'd talk to some of my friends who dabbled in real estate. A plan began to form. Whether it was a good plan remained to be seen, but at the very least I'd be able to provide stability for the current employees, though the number one person I was concerned about might not even know it was happening. "Do all the staff know?"

"Yeah. I worry about Maggie the most. She's alone and works three jobs as it is. My bartenders all have good paying day jobs, two with very flexible schedules, so even if they were let go, it wouldn't be a huge financial hardship."

We talked some more, and I reassured Pete he was doing the right thing by putting his relationship first when it mattered the most. Other people might have told him he'd waited too long, but that kind of judgment only brought more guilt and hard feelings that had no place when someone was dying. Just before Kell arrived, I slid my card to him, pointing to the private number on the back, and made him an offer on the spot. He probably would have accepted it were it not for my insistence he talk it over with his wife, or Realtor, or whoever. I wasn't going anywhere, and he needed to be sure this was what he wanted to do.

"I'm so sorry that took as long as it did, Pete. I promise I'll make up the time. Thanks for covering." Kell rang the receipts and reset the drawer.

Pete dried his hands and dropped the bag down the chute. "It was good to see you, Taylor. I'll be in touch."

"Good night, Pete, and thanks again." After he was gone, Kell tipped her head. There was a quizzical look on her face, as though she were trying to figure out what was going on.

"Glad you made it in, Kell," Jack said, serving as a distraction for us both. "Pete's great, but he draws a lousy head."

Kell laughed. "I'll be sure not to share that with him." She got a clean glass and poured a perfect two-finger head of foam. She made her way down to me and smiled. "Do you want anything else?" she asked as she took away the empty plate and utensils.

"I'm good."

Kell pursed her lips and nodded, though she looked like she wanted to say more.

"So you know about Pete selling?"

Her face fell into a frown. "Yeah. I feel bad for him. He doesn't want to lose his family's legacy, but Cassie wants him to spend time with her, and I don't blame her. If I were in her situation, I think I'd feel the same way." She wiped at imaginary spots on the bar.

"But?"

"It's selfish, but I really like this job. I hope whoever buys it keeps the staff. We may not see each other all the time, but this place is like my second home." Kell glanced around, a wistful gaze in her eyes.

"It's not selfish at all to want to keep doing what you enjoy." I drank the last in my glass and put two twenties on the bar. "I'm sure Pete will do his best to convince a potential buyer to keep the staff he has." I didn't want to go even though I'd made a commitment for a scene. What once used to hold appeal didn't thrill me anymore. "Tomorrow night you're free. Don't make plans. I'll call with instructions." I stood and leaned close enough to be heard by only Kell. "I want you to make yourself come tonight. Use whatever method you like, but I want you to scream my name and thank me when you do." I didn't wait for a response. I had Kell practicing obedience in some way every day, along with a list of chores for self-improvement and peace of mind. A good Dominant wasn't really good unless they had their submissive's best version of themself foremost as the motivation behind their actions and deeds. Anyone could demand and expect sex from their partner, but it took a special person to be a Daddy Dom, and the work involved was a reward on its own. Kell deserved the best I could provide her, and I wasn't about to give her any less.

Yet, in the back of my mind, a long-term, exclusive relationship hung, weighing heavy and keeping me grounded. I didn't know if Kell wanted that, too. At some point in the near future, I'd have to face the inevitable and have the wherewithal to find out.

CHAPTER TWENTY-FIVE

"I wasn't kidding when I said I have a play room of my own." Taylor stripped down to her jeans. Her small breasts ended in plump nipples, the dark circle surrounding them reminded me of the richest chocolate. Her feet were bare.

The room was warm. My entire body shook. No, that wasn't right. I trembled from my head to my toes. For some strange reason my mind had lost its connection with my surroundings, and I stared at the canvas slip-ons. The ones I often wore when I couldn't decide on the day's weather. When Taylor called an hour ago she told me to come over after work and not worry about dinner. I thought it was a date. Silly me. As far as I knew, which wasn't much, the people in D/s dynamics didn't date. The Dom formulated the script, the submissive obeyed, and sometimes there were scenes, play partners, and usually a whole lot of kink. I still wasn't certain of the difference between a kink and a fetish. Why did I continue to believe Taylor wanted me for herself for more than a month. I swallowed the lump. My emotions would be my undoing. Taylor would provide everything I wanted to experience. What more could I ask for?

"Take off your clothes."

Since it appeared that I'd lost my ability to speak, I toed off my shoes, glad I didn't have to use my shaking hands at the moment. I used the time to take in the space. The walls held a variety of items, including a large wardrobe unit, a couple of leather chairs, a small refrigerator, and a large-screen TV. It was dark. The beams overhead matched the others in the house with one exception. Each had a variety of thick hooks, eyes, and carabiners. In the center was a piece of leather furniture that looked like a weight bench, kind of, except it was higher off the floor and was adjustable. There was also some kind of swing, as well as a long, padded table that stood off on its own. A stainless steel cart reflected what little light there was, but what it held was covered by a dark cloth.

"All of them." Taylor stood with her legs a shoulder's width apart. There was something long and dark in her hand, but I couldn't tell what. Seconds ticked by until she made use of it by cracking the flogger across my upper thighs. Thank goodness I still had pants on. *Shit.* That explained my ass meeting the flogger.

"Yes, Sir." I was on the fast track to being naked. It's hard to know what to do with your hands when there's no place to put them, and I didn't think it would be wise to place them on my hips like an insolent child. That's how I often felt in Taylor's sophisticated presence and more so since signing our contract.

Taylor held the flogger at her side as she approached, her gaze traveling from my feet upward, pausing at my exposed pussy and then again at my breasts before holding my gaze. "Are you afraid?"

"No, Sir."

"Good." She smoothed her hand over the cheeks of my ass as she circled behind me. "Then why are you shaking?"

I took a breath, willing my body to relax. Maybe it was my mind I needed to quiet as visions of what I'd witnessed with Taylor flashed. "I don't know what to expect."

"You shouldn't expect anything. Just be in the moment."

Taylor stopped in front of me. Her face a serene mask that revealed nothing. Had she done this before? Played out a similar scene like this one so many times that it was routine?

"I am going to find out how much you want to serve me."

Her hand cupped my breast. I quietly moaned. Then she grasped my nipple, pinched it hard, and savagely twisted. My knees threatened to buckle. I tried to move back, but something in her eyes stopped me. Anything to relieve the torment. Finally, Taylor let go.

"You can make all the noises you want, but never pull away from me." She caressed my cheek, her gaze never leaving mine. "Understood?"

The pain was gone, but the implications hung on. "Yes, Sir."

She slapped the ignored breast, then yanked my nipple until I was on tiptoes. Threads of pain raced through me, and while I didn't move there was no way I could be silent. When she finished she gently rubbed both tits and the discomfort receded like an ocean wave, leaving behind the memory of it more than any real lasting effect.

"Good girl." She circled again. "There were reasons I chose you, Kell. Some I'll share with you, some I won't. The minute you signed, you gave yourself to me." She walked to a wooden stand, took something from a small dish, and returned. "On your knees." When I was in position, Taylor revealed a silver necklace with a nickel-sized circle fixed in the center. "This is a collar I bought for you. It will symbolize my ownership. I prefer it to sit at the hollow of your throat."

As she placed it at my neck, she spoke words like an oath. "By placing my collar on you, no other in the community will touch you. You are mine." She kissed my forehead, picked up her phone and took a picture. "You will look at this every morning and every night to remember who you answer to."

Afraid that I would disappoint Taylor if I remained silent, I said the only thing I thought she wanted to hear. "Yes, Sir."

"Good." Taylor nodded. "I should have done this after you signed the contract."

"Why didn't you, Sir?"

"Because whenever you wear it, I will want to be serviced."

Kell touched the symbol. "You didn't want that to happen, Sir?" She softly held my chin.

"Because you had enough to think about. I didn't want to overwhelm you." Taylor smiled

"So when do I wear it, Sir?" The metal was cold against my heated flesh.

"From the minute you rise until just before going to bed."

Maybe it should have, but it never occurred to me that I would be expected to be at Taylor's mercy when it came to sex or receiving the kind of physical satisfaction that I craved. As though knowing where my mind had gone, Taylor's fingers wrapped around my throat.

"We're going to have some fun, and you'll be a good girl for me," Taylor said.

I nodded and wondered what she considered fun. Before the night was over I was sure I'd find out. The only thing I wasn't sure of was if I would regret it.

❖

Kell looked as though she was going to throw up or pass out. I wasn't sure which was worse. I grabbed a cool washcloth and a drink with lots of electrolytes. I helped her slowly sit up and held the open bottle to her lips. "Drink some of this."

"I'm okay."

She might think she was okay, but I knew better. I'd seen a lot of sub drop in my days. I didn't consider the play we'd been having intense, however, Kell was brand new, and I should have paid more attention to her reactions to being handled roughly. It had been what *I* needed. I'd made an error thinking Kell was ready for it.

"It wasn't a suggestion." I pressed the bottle to her hand and as she drank I wiped sweat from her neck. She hadn't told me to stop, or begged, or used her safe words, which I made sure she remembered before we started. But now, as I watched her look at me with a sideways glance rather than making eye contact, I couldn't help thinking I'd somehow broken her trust. That was an outcome I hadn't expected either, nor did I want for either of us.

"Let's discuss tonight. Ask me any questions you have." I tried to sound encouraging. I'm not sure it worked. Kell continued to stare ahead, sipping water between shallow breaths. I should have corrected it, but that might push her into total silence.

"What was the spanking for, Sir? Did I do something wrong?" Kell looked extremely uncomfortable. Her face was flushed, and her hand shook a bit.

I went to the closet and brought out a robe. I draped it over her shoulders, and she slid her arms in one at a time, switching the bottle between the two like she had to have something familiar to hang on to. It gave me time to think about how I could make it clear for Kell to comprehend. "I enjoy spanking, but what I was doing was kink slapping. It's meant to sting and sometimes bruise." I took her hand. "It wasn't a punishment and I hope you enjoyed it." Last I had looked, Kell's ass was bright red. There would be bruises by morning. I thought bruises were pretty, especially on my submissive's ass and thighs. She was a blank canvas and I got to ply my brush strokes to it. The act resonated with me. "Answer me. Did you enjoy my spanking you?"

Kell took a deep breath, then let it out slowly the way I'd had her practice when she was struggling with something that was happening. "A part of me did. I got very wet."

She didn't properly address me. I wasn't going to point that out either. We were making progress. Not everything was a transgression. It was more important that Kell share her feelings with me. More corrections would make her feel as though she hadn't pleased me. She'd be wrong. Very wrong. It was natural for her to want to protect her body and I wanted her to trust that I'd never go further than I thought she could handle. If I was wrong, that meant I hadn't paid enough attention, and being careless wasn't who I'd ever been under similar circumstances. What I hadn't accounted for was Kell's silence and what it might mean. "But?"

"It…I'm not sure if I liked it enough to want it again."

It was time I took command. Kell had to always know her place and she had to be able to trust me to get her there. "You forget yourself. Address me properly or you *will* be punished."

"I'm not sure I want you to spank me like that again, Sir."

Scaring her out of wanting to continue was a consequence I wasn't willing to take. "We'll talk about it again, but not tonight." While Kell thought on that, I pulled the long ice pack from the freezer and went to the couch tucked into a corner. "Come here." I fluffed a pillow at my side. "Belly down across my lap." The uncertainty Kell had expressed had abated a bit, but as she moved into position it had renewed. "It's okay to not want everything I have to offer, but submitting to me is not negotiable."

"Yes, Sir."

I had her make an adjustment and asked if she was comfortable. Then I applied the ice over her bruised ass cheeks. With my other hand, I rubbed her back in what I hoped were soothing circles and alternately combed my fingers through her hair. It wasn't long before I felt her body relax against me. "This is one form of aftercare. You will always receive it after we have been sexually engaged or have a play session."

"That's nice," Kell mumbled into the pillow. She was quiet for a time. I had taken the opportunity to question if I was who… and what Kell needed. Maybe I'd underestimated my ability to dominate in a fashion other than for a scene or fantasy or the half-dozen other ways I got my kinks satisfied. They were all temporary. This wanting a long-term relationship with Kell was new territory for me. Maybe I didn't know how to be a partner in life. Maybe thirty days was all I'd have. If Kell wanted out, I would honor her request. A long-lasting relationship wouldn't work if I caused distrust, and right now I wasn't sure where we stood.

After I removed the ice pack, Kell rolled so she could see me. Her eyes were soft, her face relaxed. Her eyes lost their wary edge, and I breathed a little easier. Or maybe she was emotionally and physically exhausted and she had nothing left to fight with. Swallowing the bitter taste of failure as a Dominant, I needed to know how much damage I'd done. "How are you feeling now?"

"I'm not sure, Sir." Kell rose and sat next to me. "Everything happened so fast. At least, that's how it felt. I hadn't processed one thing being done before you moved onto another." She glanced at the inconspicuous clock on the wardrobe. She gave a little laugh, then shook her head. "I see now it's been a few hours, so it really wasn't that fast."

Her statement felt like barbed wire pulled along my skin. In the first two years being in the lifestyle I'd subjected myself to every imaginable toy, position, impact, play, and treatment by a Dominant who didn't have much in the way of a softer side. I was punished a lot. Depending on the person doling it out, punishment could run the gamut from pleasurable to the worst pain someone had ever experienced. She'd elicited my safe word on more than a few occasions. The good thing with my Dom was her being all about consent and safety, and she wouldn't tolerate anyone who didn't follow the rules.

I'd wanted Kell's submission so much, our play probably had gone too fast for Kell to comprehend. I might have pushed her too hard, too fast. It was a regret I'd have to live with. I couldn't apologize and seem weak or unsure of what we were doing in her eyes even if our dynamic didn't last. "It might have not gone as slow as it should have." I brushed the hair from her eyes and held her cheek. Kell leaned into my touch and a touch of hope bloomed deep inside. Maybe all wasn't lost, but I was determined to not make another blunder by wanting too much. "The next time won't be like tonight. Every time with me will be different. You were a good girl for me. I'll always take care of you."

"Who gives you aftercare, Sir?"

The breath froze in my chest. I was the one who did the caring. The one who was honored and submitted to. The one who expected unquestioned obedience. Those were the acts that had sustained me in my dynamics. I'd never thought about being cared for. I hadn't realized I wanted it…until Kell. But I couldn't confess the discovery without figuring out why. "I'm pretty self-sufficient. The only thing I need is knowing you submit because you want to, not because you have to."

"The kind of relationship you're talking about isn't at all how I pictured it would be."

"In a good way?"

"I honestly don't know, Sir."

CHAPTER TWENTY-SIX

My head pounded. The scene from two days ago lingered. Kell and I had conversed via text a number of times, though I hadn't initiated a call or discussed what had caused the confusing vibes that came from Kell.

On the one hand I'd restrained from doing all the things I wanted to tell Kell to do, as well as the things I longed to do to Kell. The visions of her tied down on a piece of my equipment and immobilizing her so she was at my mercy made me hard.

I didn't want to *have* to tie her down to have what I wanted. Kell would learn what I wanted from her, whether that be sexual or domestic would depend on my mood. Either way she'd be rewarded for unquestioning obedience. My battle had to do with whether I'd failed to be the Dominant Kell needed, and it hadn't had a cease-fire yet. I'd never questioned my motives for the things I did or how I did them because it came from the mental preparations I did prior to every interaction I had with my submissives. I saw them much as I would a child in terms of having a strong desire for reassurance and looking for guidance along their journey. Kell was childlike only in terms of her lifestyle knowledge. Outside of that existence, she was an in-charge, sure-footed woman whose confidence was a cultured and refined characteristic. How true was that juxtaposition for Kell? Would she be comfortable living the lifestyle twenty-four seven and be able to maintain her way of managing the outside world like she always had. That world…the one everyone else saw without knowledge of a living, breathing dynamic…often became unsatisfying after embracing alternate ways of looking at it. One thing was certain, I needed to find out where Kell's head was and what it meant for our dynamic.

❖

The words on the page blurred. I slipped the bookmark into the page and closed my eyes, taking a moment to be mindful of my surroundings. The softness of the pillow beneath my head. The comfortable position my body was in. The weight of the closed book on my thigh that reminded me of Kell's possessive hand there. God, that night had been intense.

The business was thriving. Wedding requests were being turned away. There were only four wedding planners, including myself on staff, and we were all running ragged with the fickle wants and needs of each bride or the families who though last-minute changes were of no consequence. Most were upper middle class or well-to-do socialites who didn't want to have to think about all the little details that went into the event. I was tired of the whole sordid rat race.

Then I remembered clients like Crystal. A woman who'd thought she was doing the right thing—the expected thing—when it wasn't what she wanted at all. We texted once or twice every week. Just a quick check in between us, though I made her promise to set a date for lunch to catch up properly. I hoped she was pursuing her authentic self. It reminded me of how Kell had resisted feelings of wanting something different, something more, for herself and not being afraid when I introduced her to the world I embraced every day.

"Hey." Les popped her head in. "Got a minute?"

"For you? Always."

"Ha, that's not what you said a few weeks ago when I handed off that delightful couple who were more interested in disagreeing than they were planning their wedding." Les shut the door and sat across from me, her features turning solemn. "There's a rumor that you're investing in another business. Is it true?"

The rumor mill worked quickly in most businesses, but ours tended to move at lightning speed because our employees were a close-knit group. "It's true. I've been wanting to delve into something I can call my own for a while now and an opportunity presented itself, though nothing is definitive yet." I should have realized that Les would be concerned if she heard. She looked uncomfortable and it wasn't a good look for her.

"Are you not happy here, Tay?"

Les rarely used the nickname she'd given me years ago. If she was using it now, she was really upset. "Of course not. If I were I hope you know I'd talk with you about it. It's just..." How could I explain the internal need for ownership of something just for me? A purpose that would feed my need to fully control something meaningful. The other motivation of wanting to ensure that Kell would be able to keep doing something she enjoyed was another important factor and one I couldn't ignore. "I'm in a new D/s dynamic and I want to have more control over things in my everyday life, as well."

"Oh." Les slid back, finally relaxing a bit into the leather chair. "That makes sense. I wish you'd talked to me though. We can rearrange the particulars of running the business so you have more say or give you the controlling ownership percentage."

"The business is fine the way it is, Les. I'm not unhappy. I need more. That's all." I thought about Melonie's family. Dale had respectfully turned down my offer of a gift of one hundred thousand dollars. I did ultimately manage to get him to agree to let me invest the money for the children's education, fifty-fifty. It wouldn't help his immediate financial struggles, but at least it would ease some of the burden down the road. I didn't have a doubt I could double the investment in five years' time, when the boy would be looking for colleges.

"My submissive works at the Water Hole. Pete, the owner, needs to focus his energy on his family so he's selling. The people he employs are good workers. It would be a shame for them to be let go just because a new owner doesn't want to inherit them." I shrugged. "I made an offer that I hope he won't turn down."

"Will you need to back off from wedding bookings to make more time for managing the Hole?"

"I don't think so, at least not in the immediate future. I also don't want to get ahead of myself. I made an offer. Nothing says he has to accept." I stood and went to the front of my desk to lean against it. "Nothing is going to change, Les, and if it does need to at some point, you'll be the first person I talk to. Okay?"

Les smiled. "Damn right you will." She stood and gave me a hug. "Be good to you. Sometimes you forget to do that." Les tapped my chest with her finger to make her point.

It was true. I took care of play partners, subs, and the business, but tending to my own needs often dropped to the bottom of the list. At one point, I thought that was the way it should be, with my focus on those I thought needed me the most, an opinion that had recently changed. "Promise."

"Good. So, when do I get to meet her?"

She never asked to meet the women I engaged with in the lifestyle. "What?"

"If you think I can't see that this mystery submissive," she said with air quotes for emphasis, "isn't someone special, you're losing your insight, my friend. You're easier to read than you once were." Les backed toward the door. "I happen to think that's a good thing."

Alone again, I played her words over in my mind. Was it that obvious that I believed Kell was more than a contracted submissive? That the more I thought about her the more I wanted a lasting relationship with her? There were worse things in the world than falling for a woman who was sexy as hell and submissive in all the ways that mattered. *Fuck.* Kell needed to know. I promised her honesty, and not telling her was a deceit I didn't want to hold on to. The only question remaining was if Kell felt the same electricity that coursed through me, but I didn't even know if she thought of me when we weren't together.

❖

Holding Kell's pussy to my face as I licked her dripping slit made my center heavy. Her head was between my thighs, her grunts and groans assuring me she was enjoying the reversed position as much as I was. I slapped her ass to stop her squirming.

"That's my good slut. Be still and take it." When she came, she drenched my chin and neck with her juices, then it was my turn. I groaned my pleasure as she kept licking before finally collapsing against me. I held her there, rubbing her body, enjoying the smooth skin beneath my palms.

"Oh, God." Kell's head rested on my center.

After waiting a couple of beats, I smacked her ass hard three times, and she jerked to attention.

"Thank you, Sir."

I smoothed her pink ass. "Don't forget next time." Not that I think she needed the warning, but she was still learning about my requirements for respect and gratitude. It was a hard lesson to learn, but necessary. She had to know her place. "Come here." She moved into my arms. "You did well. I want you to behave for me." I lifted her chin to see her eyes. The haze was gone. "Understand?"

"Yes, Sir."

"Good. Let's shower. There's something we need to talk about." I took her hand and led the way. "Fix the temperature, then get water." She did as I instructed, then followed me into the steamy water. I soaped the cloth and washed her with care. "My turn," I said as I handed her the cloth. Kell soaped it and thoroughly washed away the sticky juices. We dried and then dressed in soft, casual clothes. I'd be tempted to take her again if I had quick access to her, so it was best that she wore pants.

"I'll fix us a drink and meet you on the porch."

She hesitated for a brief instant. "Yes, Sir."

As I mixed cocktails, I thought about the surging pressure in my crotch that I had no desire to address. Perhaps later there'd be a reason to celebrate. If not, I'd quiet the beast inside one way or another.

Kell was in one of the padded chairs, her eyes closed, her breathing deep. She looked calm. I was pleased with her demeanor. I set the tumbler down and took the other chair as quietly as possible. Her eyes fluttered open.

"Sorry, Sir." She straightened in her seat.

I placed my hand on her arm to reassure her. "It's good to relax. I'm not an ogre." I chuckled and she settled against the back of the chair. I handed her drink to her.

After a sip, she faced me. "You wanted to talk? Sir."

"You can drop the formality for now." There was both dread and anticipation coursing through my veins. The hope that she wanted the same things I want from our dynamic may not be possible, but with dedication we'd both be satisfied. "What do you want out of our relationship, Kell?"

"I'm not sure what you mean." She ran her fingertip along the beveled edge of the glass.

"Are you experimenting to see if you like the lifestyle? In it to make your fantasies come to fruition? What's your motivation?" I didn't want to rush her into providing an answer she might not be sure of. She sipped her drink and glanced off in the distance. I sat back, content to wait.

When she finally looked up her gaze met mine without any hesitation. "I was instantly attracted to you." Kell's mouth twitched at one corner. "Then you pissed me off." She laughed. "That was before I realized what a complicated personality you were, and I began to appreciate that your manners, your behavior, weren't anything at all like I was used to. I'd met egotistical, overconfident women most of my life. You weren't like that. You were...you. Charming, unexpected. You caught me off guard and surprised me a dozen times. I wasn't sure how to handle what you were offering, especially when you said I'd have to trust you." She drank a bit more, set her glass down, then pulled one leg up on her seat and hugged it.

"That's nice to hear, but it doesn't answer any of my questions."

She rested her head on her knee as she stared at me. "You're used to getting what you want when you want it."

The statement wasn't wrong, but I had no idea Kell would be brave enough to speak it. "Most of the time."

"But I'm not likely to bend to anyone's will, though I did wonder what it would feel like if I did. What would happen if

I abandoned the control I'd survived on my whole life? That's where you got my attention. Suddenly it was very clear how living in a controlled bubble was stifling so much of what I wanted to try and explore and experience." Kell's head came up, her eyes sparkling with excitement. "Then we went to the bar and the things I saw blew my mind."

"I hope in a good way." I worried, had from the first night, that it was too much for Kell to process and I'd scare her from taking a chance she might actually like some of the things that were happening.

"Oh yeah. Like I understood. The people with cuffs and collars and harnesses, they're people, just like me. There were probably doctors, lawyers, teachers, and every other profession. People embracing their uniqueness and their particular way of expressing their sexual desires. Their..." She tipped her head back the way I'd often seen her do when she was in deep thought. "Their kinks and fetishes." Kell giggled quietly. "I'm still not sure of the difference, but I'll get there. You gave me things to read to help me understand. To show me how different a dynamic was from the run-of-the-mill relationship. Nothing was clandestine or secretive. Everything was out in the open, which left no room for deception or misunderstanding. It was so different from everything I thought I knew about being a couple." Kell took a breath and grinned. "I'm rambling." Her cheeks colored as she finished her drink.

"Not at all. I've been in the lifestyle so long I forgot how eye-opening that first brush with a world so different from the one I walked through every day felt. Thank you for reminding me."

"You're welcome, Sir." Kell playfully batted her eyes.

"Don't push it." I said it with a serious tone that left no room for misinterpretation. Inside, I was laughing out loud.

Kell cast her eyes downward. "Sorry."

"Did you forget something?"

Dawning flashed in her eyes. "Sorry, Sir."

"Better." I almost left it at that, but I couldn't. I had to know more. Had to know how Kell felt on the inside regarding the lifestyle I wanted to live all day, every day. "Does that mean what we're doing is an experiment?" Disappointment and anger rose, fighting for supremacy. How would she answer? The question burned through me like a branding iron.

Kell nearly jumped out of her seat. "No!" She took a minute to regain her composure. "I might not understand everything that happens, or why, but that doesn't mean I don't want to learn."

"All you need to do is ask." That was the caveat of strained relationships. One person did not trust the other enough to ask the hard questions without being ridiculed or brushed off. Or even worse, ignored. What were people afraid of?

"That's the ultimate form of trust, isn't it? To be able to ask anything and knowing that the answer is the other person's truth is kind of amazing."

"Yes, it is." I leaned closer. "What's your truth, Kell?" The terror in her eyes betrayed her. She was still afraid to share her truth with me. My heart sank. Maybe she would always hold back, unable to trust me the way I wanted her to. It wasn't something I could force, not that I'd even try.

"I…I'm not sure." She looked crestfallen.

I felt the palpable shame surrounding the reality that she couldn't fully open herself up to me. I wasn't willing to push for answers she didn't have because I knew I would be disappointed if I did. That wasn't how I dealt with a hesitant submissive and that's what Kell was. Somehow, I'd failed to provide the security she needed to bear her soul, and the knife wound the admission left behind would lead to my bleeding out if I didn't fix it. "I want you to think about the question. We'll discuss it again." I stood and held out my hand. "But right now, we're going to go visit someone."

Kell took my hand, confusion written in her eyes. "Where are we going?"

"If I tell you, it will ruin the surprise."

CHAPTER TWENTY-SEVEN

Taylor insisted I didn't need to change clothes, but when we pulled up to the Hole I glanced down and cringed. "What are we doing here?"

"It's where the surprise is." She pulled the key and got out, practically running around the car to get to my door.

"Taylor, are you going to tell me what's going on?" I swallowed hard. This Taylor, the bubbly, excited person standing next to me, wasn't a Taylor I was familiar with. It was a little disconcerting.

"Soon. I promise."

She took my hand and led me to the door, then opened it and waved me inside. It took a quick look around to realize all my co-workers and my boss, Pete, were there. So was Jack who looked like the Cheshire Cat, big smile and all. I whipped around to face Taylor. "What is going on?" I hissed the words.

"Kell," Pete said. "Why don't you come belly up to the bar and let me make you a drink in celebration."

I pursed my lips and slid onto a stool. Everyone was smiling, but my gut told me there was a foreboding that hung in the air, thick and heavy like the smog in LA. Pete slid a lychee martini in front of me. He slid a drink to Taylor.

"Okay, everybody. Raise your glasses. It's my distinct pleasure to introduce you to the new owner of the Water Hole, Taylor Simpson." Cheers went out as everyone drank.

"I don't understand." The whole thing felt surreal. "What?" I shook my head. "How is that possible?" There was only one person who could tell me the whole story and I turned to Taylor again, looking for answers.

"I promise to tell you everything. Let's enjoy the celebration, shall we?"

I blinked in disbelief. Taylor was not only my Dominant, she was apparently also my new boss. Could this night get any stranger? "You better," I said, then added, "Sir." As I looked around the space there were animated conversations happening in groups of two or three people. There were more people than the employees alone. It appeared Pete had expanded the celebration to include partners. That was sweet, even if I didn't have a partner. Was Taylor my partner? No, that wasn't right. Taylor was my Dom. We had a contract. Even if I'd been entertaining having more with her, it was pretty clear Taylor didn't want more.

Taylor climbed up on the bar and the hoots and hollers seemed to encourage her. Not that she needed it. "As the new owner, I want you all to know no one is losing their job." The cacophony of noise rose to a deafening level. Taylor got the crowd to quiet. "I'm also going to hire a few more people to give you some well-deserved time off. I don't want anyone to burn out. Lastly, I want to thank Pete for trusting me with his family's business." She turned to Pete. "I promise to carry on some of the traditions that have been in place for decades." She lifted her glass and tapped Pete's. I didn't miss the tears in his eyes as he nodded his thanks. She jumped down and came to my side. I stared at her.

"What?"

"You never cease to amaze me. How is that possible?"

"It's a secret."

I laughed. "Another one?"

"Yes. There's one more, but I have to tell you in private."

I didn't want to wait. Taylor had a way of leading me into a state of excitement like no one ever had. "Let's go."

"No. We're going to stay and celebrate with Pete. He deserves his freedom, and his wife is ecstatic." She looked around. "So are your co-workers."

My gaze followed hers. She was right, and I was happy for each person. "I'm glad you gave them all peace of mind."

"What about you? Are you happy about the change?"

Was I? Did I want to answer to Taylor in and out of our dynamic? Maybe a little piece of me worried over the addition of being under Taylor's thumb even more, but if anyone was going to be able to make it work, she was the one to do it. "Yes, I am."

Taylor nodded. "Good." Taylor moved around the room, introducing herself to the staff and asking questions about what they did and how things might be better. She was attentive and sincere. The more I watched her, the more I appreciated her. It was almost midnight by the time we said our good-byes. Pete would hand off the keys sometime tomorrow and make the switch official.

"Ready to know the other secret?"

I was beginning to think she wasn't going to ever tell me. I jumped up. "Yes, Sir."

"Eager slut." Taylor whispered the words in my ear.

The degree that it was true had been a total shock to me, but I was beginning to enjoy it more and more. "Yes, Sir." I couldn't wait to find out what other news Taylor had to tell me.

❖

We sat on the bed facing each other. My heart pounded in my chest as I tried to figure out what was so important that Taylor needed to tell me privately.

"Every once in a while, life throws us a curve ball and we can either duck and let it sail over our head, or we can stick our hand out and catch it. Take a chance on the unknown."

She wasn't making any sense; it wasn't like her to not clearly speak her mind. What could possibly be so terrible she didn't know how to tell me? Oh, God. She had another submissive. Was that it? Was I just one among however many? I wasn't special after all. I began to shake. If that was true, there wasn't anything I could do to change the situation. Taylor did what she wanted when she wanted. I had no control except to tap out. My heart was beating so hard in my chest it was going to explode. It was a real possibility. I had to get out of there.

"I get it. You've got another submissive." I said the words casually, but I was crushed. We'd only been in a dynamic a few weeks and I had already lost my place, not worth the time and effort it would take to train me to be what she wanted. I pushed up, Taylor grabbed my wrist.

"No, no. That's not it, Kell. You couldn't be any more off base."

I dropped to the bed, the strength I usually relied on was gone. I'd deal with whatever news Taylor was determined to tell me and lick my wounds later. I was good at recovering from disappointment.

"The contract that you and I signed isn't necessary because I want more. More than a month, or two, or three with you. I want you for my submissive in life."

"I don't know what that means."

Taylor took a breath. "Sometimes a dynamic turns into a lifetime relationship. That's what I want with you, but it won't work for either of us if you don't want it, too. After our conversation the other day, I was convinced I'd made a mistake thinking you were as into me as I was into you. It didn't matter. I couldn't give up that easily. I couldn't survive not knowing if I was making an assumption, or if what I felt was real." Taylor held my hand to her chest. "Is it real, Kell? Do you have feelings that go deeper than any piece of paper might tell us to honor?"

The plea in Taylor's eyes was genuine. If I understood correctly, she wanted us to enter into a lifetime dynamic. One where she was the Dominant and I was the submissive above and beyond the boundaries set forth by each other. That we would grow in the dynamic and nurture each other in ways traditional relationships never could.

"I've been wondering why I was so confused about what was between us, and now I know. I love you because of who you are and because you want the best for me, in spite of me not realizing my potential. If that isn't love, I don't know what is."

Taylor closed the short gap between us. "I don't have experience with love outside of a dynamic, but if there's anyone who can help me fulfill my dreams and fantasies and all the dirty, kinky things I want to enjoy, I know that person is you."

I brought her hands to my lips. "That's something I definitely want, Sir." I looked up through my lashes. "When can we get started, Sir?"

Taylor cupped my cheek. "On your knees, slut. That's where you start."

Wet heat coated my thighs. If it was any indication of how much I was invested, I was all in for whatever Taylor had in mind for us. I had a feeling we'd learn as we went, and I was more than happy to let Taylor lead me wherever her dominance led.

"Yes, Sir. As you wish."

About the Author

Renee Roman lives in upstate New York with her fur baby, Maisie. She is blessed by close friends and a supportive family. She is passionate about many things including living an adventurous life, exploring her authentic self, and writing lesbian romance and erotica.

Her novel *Body Language* was a 2022 GCLS finalist. Her latest works include *Escorted* and *Glass and Stone*. All of her books can be found at Bold Strokes Books and everywhere books are sold.

You can catch up with Renee on Facebook and Twitter. She'd love to hear from you by emailing her at reneeromanwrites@gmail.com

Books Available from Bold Strokes Books

Before She Was Mine by Emma L McGeown. When Dani and Lucy are thrust together to sort out their children's playground squabble, sparks fly leaving both of them willing to risk it all for each other. 978-1-63679-315-3)

Chasing Cypress by Ana Hartnett Reichardt. Maggie Hyde wants to find a partner to settle down with and help her run the family farm, but instead she ends up chasing Cypress. Olivia Cypress. 978-1-63679-323-8)

Dark Truths by Sandra Barret. When Jade's ex-girlfriend and vampire maker barges back into her life, can Jade satisfy her ex's demands, keep Beth safe, and keep everyone's secrets… secret? 978-1-63679-369-6)

Desires Unleashed by Renee Roman. Kell Murphy and Taylor Simpson didn't go looking for love, but as they explore their desires unleashed, their hearts lead them on an unexpected journey. 978-1-63679-327-6)

Maybe, Probably by Amanda Radley. Set against the backdrop of a viral pandemic, Gina and Eleanor are about to discover that loving another person is complicated when you're desperately searching for yourself. 978-1-63679-284-2)

The One by C.A. Popovich. Jody Acosta doesn't know what makes her more furious, that the wealthy Bergeron family refuses to be held accountable for her father's wrongful death, or that she can't ignore her knee-weakening attraction to Nicole Bergeron. 978-1-63679-318-4)

The Speed of Slow Changes by Sander Santiago. As Al and Lucas navigate the ups and downs of their polyamorous relationship, only one thing is certain: romance has never been so crowded. 978-1-63679-329-0)

Tides of Love by Kimberly Cooper Griffin. Falling in love is the last thing on either of their minds, but when Mikayla and Gem meet, sparks of possibility begin to shine, revealing a future neither expected. 978-1-63679-319-1)

Catch by Kris Bryant. Convincing the wife of the star quarterback to walk away from her family was never in offensive coordinator Sutton McCoy's game plan. But standing on the sidelines when a second chance at true love comes her way proves all but impossible. (978-1-63679-276-7)

Hearts in the Wind by MJ Williamz. Beth and Evelyn seem destined to remain mortal enemies but are about to discover that in matters of the heart, sometimes you must cast your fortunes to the wind. (978-1-63679-288-0)

Hero Complex by Jesse J. Thoma. Bronte, Athena, and their unlikely friends, must work together to defeat Bronte's arch nemesis. The fate of love, humanity, and the world might depend on it. No pressure. (978-1-63679-280-4)

Hotel Fantasy by Piper Jordan. Molly Taylor has a fantasy in mind that only Lexi can fulfill. However, convincing her to participate could prove challenging. (978-1-63679-207-1)

Last New Beginning by Krystina Rivers. Can commercial broker Skye Kohl and contractor Bailey Kaczmarek overcome their pride and work together while the tension between them boils over into a love that could soothe both of their hearts? (978-1-63679-261-3)

Love and Lattes by Karis Walsh. Cat café owner Bonnie and wedding planner Taryn join forces to get rescue cats into forever homes—discovering their own forever along the way. (978-1-63679-290-3)

Repatriate by Jaime Maddox. Ally Hamilton's new job as a home health aide takes an unexpected twist when she discovers a fortune in stolen artwork and must repatriate the masterpieces and avoid the wrath of the violent man who stole them. (978-1-63679-303-0)

The Hues of Me and You by Morgan Lee Miller. Arlette Adair and Brooke Dawson almost fell in love in college. Years later, they unexpectedly run into each other and come face-to-face with their unresolved past. (978-1-63679-229-3)

A Haven for the Wanderer by Jenny Frame. When Griffin Harris comes to Rosebrook village, the love she finds with Bronte de Lacey creates safe haven and she finally finds her place in the world. But will she run again when their love is tested? (978-1-63679-291-0)

A Spark in the Air by Dena Blake. Internet executive Crystal Tucker is sure Wi-Fi could really help small-town residents, even if it means putting an internet café out of business, but her instant attraction to the owner's daughter, Janie Elliott, makes moving ahead with her plans complicated. (978-1-63679-293-4)

Between Takes by CJ Birch. Simone Lavoie is convinced her new job as an intimacy coordinator will give her a fresh perspective. Instead, problems on set and her growing attraction to actress Evelyn Harper only add to her worries. (978-1-63679-309-2)

Camp Lost and Found by Georgia Beers. Nobody knows better than Cassidy and Frankie that life doesn't always give you what you want. But sometimes, if you're lucky, life gives you exactly what you need. (978-1-63679-263-7)

Felix Navidad by 'Nathan Burgoine. After the wedding of a good friend, instead of Felix's Hawaii Christmas treat to himself, ice rain strands him in Ontario with fellow wedding-guest—and handsome ex of said friend—Kevin in a small cabin for the holiday Felix definitely didn't plan on. (978-1-63679-411-2)

Fire, Water, and Rock by Alaina Erdell. As Jess and Clare reveal more about themselves, and their hot summer fling tips over into true love, they must confront their pasts before they can contemplate a future together. (978-1-63679-274-3)

Lines of Love by Brey Willows. When even the Muse of Love doesn't believe in forever, we're all in trouble. (978-1-63555-458-8)

Manny Porter and The Yuletide Murder by D.C. Robeline. Manny only has the holiday season to discover who killed prominent research scientist Phillip Nikolaidis before the judicial system condemns an innocent man to lethal injection. (978-1-63679-313-9)

Only This Summer by Radclyffe. A fling with Lily promises to be exactly what Chase is looking for—short-term, hot as a forest fire, and one Chase can extinguish whenever she wants. After all, it's only one summer. (978-1-63679-390-0)

Picture-Perfect Christmas by Charlotte Greene. Two former rivals compete to capture the essence of their small mountain town at Christmas, all the while fighting old and new feelings. (978-1-63679-311-5)

Playing Love's Refrain by Lesley Davis. Drew Dawes had shied away from the world of music until Wren Banderas gave her a reason to play their love's refrain. (978-1-63679-286-6)

Profile by Jackie D. The scales of justice are weighted against FBI agents Cassidy Wolf and Alex Derby. Loyalty and love may be the only advantage they have. (978-1-63679-282-8)

Almost Perfect by Tagan Shepard. A shared love of queer TV brings Olivia and Riley together, but can they keep their real-life love as picture perfect as their on-screen counterparts? (978-1-63679-322-1)

Corpus Calvin by David Swatling. Cloverkist Inn may be haunted, but a ghost materializes from Jason Dekker's past and Calvin's canine instinct kicks in to protect a young boy from mortal danger. (978-1-62639-428-5)

Craving Cassie by Skye Rowan. Siobhan Carney and Cassie Townsend share an instant attraction, but are they brave enough to give up everything they have ever known to be together? (978-1-63679-062-6)

Drifting by Lyn Hemphill. When Tess jumps into the ocean after Jet, she thinks she's saving her life. Of course, she can't possibly know Jet is actually a mermaid desperate to fix her mistake before she causes her clan's demise. (978-1-63679-242-2)

Enigma by Suzie Clarke. Polly has taken an oath to protect and serve her country, but when the spy she's tasked with hunting becomes the love of her life, will she be the one to betray her country? (978-1-63555-999-6)

Finding Fault by Annie McDonald. Can environmental activist Dr. Evie O'Halloran and government investigator Merritt Shepherd set aside their conflicting ideas about saving the planet and risk their hearts enough to save their love? (978-1-63679-257-6)

Hot Keys by R.E. Ward. In 1920s New York City, Betty May Dewitt and her best friend, Jack Norval, are determined to make their Tin Pan Alley dreams come true and discover they will have to fight—not only for their hearts and dreams, but for their lives. (978-1-63679-259-0)

Securing Ava by Anne Shade. Private investigator Paige Richards takes a case to locate and bring back runaway heiress Ava Prescott. But ignoring her attraction may prove impossible when their hearts and lives are at stake. (978-1-63679-297-2)

The Amaranthine Law by Gun Brooke. Tristan Kelly is being hunted for who she is and her incomprehensible past, and despite her overwhelming feelings for Olivia Bryce, she has to reject her to keep her safe. (978-1-63679-235-4)

The Forever Factor by Melissa Brayden. When Bethany and Reid confront their past, they give new meaning to letting go, forgiveness, and a future worth fighting for. (978-1-63679-357-3)

The Frenemy Zone by Yolanda Wallace. Ollie Smith-Nakamura thinks relocating from San Francisco to her dad's rural hometown is the worst idea in the world, but after she meets her new classmate Ariel Hall, she might have a change of heart. (978-1-63679-249-1)

A Cutting Deceit by Cathy Dunnell. Undercover cop Athena takes a job at Valeria's hair salon to gather evidence to prove her husband's connections to organized crime. What starts as a tentative friendship quickly turns into a dangerous affair. (978-1-63679-208-8)

As Seen on TV! by CF Frizzell. Despite their objections, TV hosts Ronnie Sharp, a laid-back chef; and paranormal investigator Peyton Stanford, have to work together. The public is watching. But joining forces is risky, contemptuous, unnerving, provocative—and ridiculously perfect. (978-1-63679-272-9)

Blood Memory by Sandra Barret. Can vampire Jade Murphy protect her friend from a human stalker and keep her dates with the gorgeous Beth Jenssen without revealing her secrets? (978-1-63679-307-8)

Foolproof by Leigh Hays. For Martine Roberts and Elliot Tillman, friends with benefits isn't a foolproof way to hide from the truth at the heart of an affair. (978-1-63679-184-5)

Glass and Stone by Renee Roman. Jordan must accept that she can't control everything that happens in life, and that includes her wayward heart. (978-1-63679-162-3)

Hard Pressed by Aurora Rey. When rivals Mira Lavigne and Dylan Miller are tapped to co-chair Finger Lakes Cider Week, competition gives way to compromise. But will their sexual chemistry lead to love? (978-1-63679-210-1)

The Laws of Magic by M. Ullrich. Nothing is ever what it seems, especially not in the small town of Bender, Massachusetts, where a witch lives to save lives and avoid love. (978-1-63679-222-4)

The Lonely Hearts Rescue by Morgan Lee Miller, Nell Stark, Missouri Vaun. In this novella collection, a hurricane hits the Gulf Coast, and the animals at the Lonely Hearts Rescue Shelter need love, and so do the humans who adopt them. (978-1-63679-231-6)

The Mage and the Monster by Barbara Ann Wright. Two powerful mages, one committed to magic and one controlled by it, strive to free each other and be together while the countries they serve descend into war. (978-1-63679-190-6)

Truly Wanted by J.J. Hale. Sam must decide if she's willing to risk losing her found family to find her happily ever after. (978-1-63679-333-7)